LIFT

LIFT

A MEMOIR BY

Rebecca K. O'Connor

 RED HEN PRESS | *Los Angeles, CA*

Lift
Copyright © 2009 by Rebecca K. O'Connor

Book layout by Sydney Nichols

ISBN: 978-1-59709-460-3
Library of Congress Catalog Card Number: 2009928522

The Annenberg Foundation, the James Irvine Foundation, the Los Angeles County Arts Commission, and the National Endowment for the Arts partially support Red Hen Press.

First Edition

Published by Red Hen Press
www.redhen.org

Excerpts of this memoir have been published in the *California Hawking Club Journal*, the *North American Falconers Association Journal*, *West*, *South Dakota Review*, *Iron Horse Literary Review*, *divide*, and *Narrative*.

The following organizations have supported this project through fellowships: the Albert and Elaine Borchard Fellowship to the Tomales Bay Writers' Workshops, the Carlisle Family Scholarship to the Community of Writers at Squaw Valley workshops, fellowship to the San Juan Writers' Workshops, and the McQuern Fellowship in nonfiction at the University of California, Riverside. Thank you all for believing in my work.

My thanks go to friends, family, peers, and mentors who have supported the writing and the often-difficult journey of this project. I couldn't have done it without you.

Most especially, thank you to the falconers and biologists who brought the peregrine back from the brink of North American extinction. Equally, thanks to the sportsmen, sportswomen, conservationists, and scientists who continue to fight for waterfowl and wetlands preservation. Without organizations like the Peregrine Fund and Ducks Unlimited, this story would have ended before it started.

Contents

Remember, my son, that the only healthy way to live is out in the open air and daylight, that everything deprived of freedom loses its identity and soon dies. This little book on falconry will teach you to appreciate the life of the open field.

—*Count Alphonse de Toulouse,*
in a dedication penned in his son,
Henri de Toulouse-Lautrec's copy of the
Small Handbook on Falconry *(1876)*

I should kill the duck. I know how to do it. A master falconer showed me with a deft hand. He split the skin where the leg meets the body and with his finger hooked, jammed it inside and found the heart. It dislodged with no sound and laid beating in his palm. He offered it with an open hand to my falcon who took it with dainty bites while the duck stilled.

The falconer gauged my expression, wondering if I thought my fingers could do the same. I met his eyes and nodded that I could. I had been a falconer myself for eight years. I flew my falcon nearly every day, keeping his wingbeat strong and his heart wild. I slogged through mud and splashed into ponds, a bird dog for a duck-hunting falcon. I was determined to do my job. I had asked the falconer if he knew a quick way to kill a duck bound tight in the talon-tipped feet of a falcon. If what he had shown me was mercy, then it's what I would do.

I tried it myself several weeks later, but found that my hands were too small and clumsy. I couldn't find the grape-sized heart, and when finally, I did, I couldn't free it from the hollow of the duck's chest. It beat against my fingers and I wondered what kind of a monster I was, a failure of a predator, unable to dispatch my prey with casual quickness. I should kill this duck, but once again, I'm a failure.

Sometimes my peregrine falcon cuts through a flock of ducks, diving from a thousand feet. With two seconds to choose through a view that must be blurred with the speed, he picks a duck that stands out in its weak or uncertain wingbeat. These flights are an audible battle, the wind complaining through the falcon's feathers and bell with the same concern it gives artillery. When the falcon connects a high-speed dive, a stoop like this, there is no beating heart to seek with shaking fingers; the duck remains a piece of the sky and only its body careens to the earth. That's when I love a peregrine's flight, when it is serious and merciful.

My peregrine is rarely serious and never merciful. By now he understands that a forceful blow is neat, clean and so much easier. Yet he takes a meal however he can get it even if he has to rip a duck from the sky and brawl like a graceless mammal on the ground. I've seen him tackle a drake mallard four times his size and win, but not without a price. He has cracked the critical flight feathers at the edges of his wings. I have seen a duck rip the central feather from his tail with the tip of its webbed foot. The broken feathers will come back new with the next season, but the tail feather may never grow back. Feathers are crucial and protected by their flexible strength, but can only withstand so much life-desperate prey. The peregrine chooses messy battles and I believe I have no choice but to be in the middle of them.

The ducks are safe on the pond. They are only vulnerable in the air where they can be spun by a hunter's gun or struck by a stooping falcon. They understand this even in their first migration down the Pacific Flyway. So when my falcon flies and climbs to a pitch of a thousand feet above the pond, I see it is my job to put the ducks in harm's way. They bob in the water, their invisible feet paddling them into tight circles as their dark blinking eyes sneak quick glimpses above, and no amount of yelling and rock throwing will bring them to split their bodies from the water.

When my bird is so high that searching the sky for him gives me vertigo, that is when I feel most obligated by our bond. He believes I will make the ducks come off the pond. Even when he's nothing more than a flashing speck momentarily visible against the cloud-line, we are still an inseparable team. I've worked hard to convince him this is true and he has worked hard to gain the thick breast muscles that allow him to mount the sky. There's only forty feet between the ducks and me, a short swim that seems incomparable to the peregrine's climb. It's the least I can do. If he flies well, I always flush the ducks.

Today I didn't have to swim. The duck that is now cinched in the falcon's feet came off the pond cleanly, a nervously powerful straight arrow flight. Sometimes the ducks hug the edge of the pond, drawing the falcon in and when the power of his stoop is wasted, splash back into safety. The peregrine knows these tricks now. He won't waste his pitch on a duck that hasn't reached the open. It didn't matter. This duck didn't bother with trickery. I watched it bolt off the water with so much grace and power I believed in the duck and doubted my falcon.

Even as a connoisseur of warm-blooded flight, I couldn't have designed a more perfect bird than a duck. I love the decadence of their down and the impossible colors of a breeding drake. I admire the wiles of the teal and how they randomly scatter at just a glimpse of my smile. I love the way the mallards are brazen enough to always leave the ponds first without looking over their shoulders and how the pintails wait for the other ducks to focus the falcon like a heat-seeking missile and then slip quietly out the back way. I love it when the ducks get away, although, I love it more when they don't.

Today's duck was bigger than a teal or even a gadwall, bigger than a lazy mallard living on palm-fed cracked corn. It rose from the pond, powering for the horizon, without a glance at the falcon above it. The peregrine hesitated only long enough for the duck's shadow to appear gliding across the ground and then he tucked into a dive. I watched my bird fall with all the momentum his little body could gain from his six-hundred-foot pitch and make contact with audible force. It was only enough of a blow to nudge the large duck into the ground, merging with its shadow, and though it bounced with the meeting the duck still got up again, the falcon close behind. I lost sight of the two opponents and scrambled through the creosote to find them. The duck looked too heavy to regain the air and I knew that the peregrine would not relinquish any hold he might manage. I wondered what species of duck I had flushed. I didn't get a good enough look at it to be sure, but thought it had the drab colors of a female.

I found the falcon and the duck at the fence line and wondered if the mystery duck had drug him there. The delicate feathers and gentle eyes of a duck in repose hide its sharp hard bones and commitment to staying alive. I've seen a duck drag the peregrine across a field of close-cropped alfalfa, whipping its wings in an attempt to knock death off its back. Waterfowl will roll, kick, and struggle back to the water where a falcon might be drowned. These tactics occasionally leave the falcon with nothing more than a scatter of lost feathers surrounding his feet, stunned and unsteady, still standing where the duck broke free. The peregrine could get badly hurt in a losing battle, but he's learned that I'll get there and turn the tide. I protect the falcon, but when I step in, I'm also responsible for the duck.

Now my falcon's beak and chest feathers are dipped in blood and his eyes wild. His wings and tail are in disarray and I know I have missed the real battle, but am thankful not to have to reach in between them at their full strength. The duck has lost, but still weakly kicks and struggles.

I untangle their wings and let my falcon stand upright, examining their engagement. The duck is three times the size of my falcon. The long yellow toes of the peregrine's delicate feet are wrapped securely around his prey's head and neck. I wince at the talon in the duck's eye and the spot where he has flayed her open to eat, wishing he had killed her outright. There is no way to break the duck's neck without wringing my falcon in the process.

I know I should kill the duck, but I don't want to fumble with its insides. The peregrine revels in the taste of blood from her neck, and I know this is greater torture than attempted mercy from me, but I can't do it.

Instead, I look over the duck, stroking her wing and burying my fingers in her thick feathers. I still don't know what sort of duck this is. I wonder if it's a redhead, examining its rusty brown head and trying not to look in its one good eye. Admiring the delicate grey pattern of its back, I decide it must be a gadwall and not a hen at all, but a drake. However, it seems too heavy and its tail too short and I don't see the white speculum. I don't know what species of duck this is, and when I step my falcon off of it, finally wringing its neck, I can't even thank it by name.

Walking back to the truck, the duck in my bag, I don't feel elated. The peregrine rides on my glove, picking the last bits of food off his toes, his eyes almond-shaped and the beard of feathers beneath his chin puffed out against the early sun. My falcon is as pleased as I have ever seen him and deserves to be, but the weight of the duck tucked in the voluminous back pocket of my vest pulls against my shoulders and feels too much like guilt.

My hands are painted in duck blood, but there's a hollowness in my chest where my pride should be. It's been a hard journey gaining this falcon's trust, convincing him to hunt with me, but I still wonder if I'm hunter or prey. I still wonder what it means to be partner to a peregrine.

PART I

Chapter One

My Mother's Daughter

My mom is a little drunk. I can tell this in one spoken word, in the way she clips "hi" into a false syllable of cheer. She's not an alcoholic, but this has somehow become our new ritual, getting drunk across the phone lines. So much has changed recently. We drink because the change is good and because it scares us.

I've only just picked up the phone, but before I can falsify my own greeting, the African grey parrot has answered "Hi, Mom," for me, a perfectly nuanced rendition of my voice emanating from the far corner of the living room. I sound happy that she called.

"Ty says hi," I say and start rummaging for a bottle opener in the confusion of the kitchen utensil drawer. "Despite what the parrot says, you're not the only person who calls me."

"I know that." She answers the way a mother should, even though we both know it's not exactly true. Parrots don't lie. "Adam calls, right?" She asks, knowing I must talk to my boyfriend on the phone.

"Sometimes," I answer a little defensively. The truth is, mostly, I call him and I haven't talked to him in a week. "How are you?" I ask, even though I know, even though I don't want to hear more. What I really want to do is down a glass or two of Charles Shaw merlot and catch up. It's nerve-grating, talking to her when she's drunk and I'm sober.

I'm only half-listening to her while I open the bottle and start on my first glass. I know we have to get this part of the conversation out of the way, a few minutes of complaint about her life before we can move on to philosophy and hope. I need to listen for a while to how my stepfather stole twenty-six years of her life. She needs to share his latest disturbing attempt to get her back, his veiled threat to her about the dangers of living alone, a plea to her to think of the family, or a profession of his pure, undying love. His every attempt is stranger and more futile because we know now that he is the danger, that he doesn't really understand love and he's had another family, a wife and two kids, hidden away off the coast of Seattle for seventeen years.

Mom says friends tell her she should sell her story, that she should sue him. She's afraid someone might discover our delicious family drama and we could all end up shamed on Jerry Springer. I don't have the heart to tell her that her story is more cliché than drama. As far as I can see, this is the way of the world. Predator or prey, you choose.

I don't know why she makes the choices that she does. I want to think that I'm not my mother, that I would have seen that man for who he was, past the cloak of sheepskin and noticed the sharp teeth in his smile. The truth is, though, that I didn't. I too saw his blue eyes, shining with concern, admired his close-cropped beard and wire-rimmed glasses. I wanted to believe he was intelligent and kind. I wanted him to love me too.

"I'm sorry," I tell her. It's a reply more to the tone of her voice than her words. What did she say? Something about how she thinks now that they were never married. She doesn't think he filed the license. My mother left me for a man who didn't even make their marriage legal and who only gave her and her other children half of what they deserved. And what about what I deserved? My mind wanders while my mother talks.

🦆

I'm three years old and something has bitten into the arch of my foot. It hurts. Not like a scraped knee or a bumped elbow, but in a way that rings up my leg and buzzes all the way to my fingernails.

I'm in the enclosed patio on the red concrete floor, tilting my back against the pool table. I twist my leg to look at the bottom of my foot. I examine the stain of dirt and blue dust that rings the outside of my heel. A steady ooze of sticky crimson collects and drips from the bend of my small foot. In the center of the wetness something shimmers in the light. I touch it and a shock of pain makes me kick. There is something lodged deep in the skin. I shriek.

My mother pushes through the sliding glass door and scoops me up, examining the blood and already cooing that I'll be alright, that she'll fix me right up.

"She's got a piece of glass in her foot, Barry." My father joins her at the sink as my mom yanks the curve of glass free and the blood flows faster. She holds it up for him to examine.

"Tell her to quit crying. She's fine," he says and I cry harder.

My mom's hands are gentle and she speaks to me like she would speak to an adult, explaining why it's okay, saying that it will quit hurting in a moment, reasoning with me that it is only a cut and that cuts heal. Her voice is just a murmur of words. I don't make sense of them. It's the feel of her arms around me that is soothing, her dark thick hair falling in my face. My foot aches, but everything is better.

"So what's going on with you?" Mom finishes her story and exhales this question with a sigh. I rub at the arch of my foot where I can feel the ridge of a scar that is nearly as old as I am. Everything is changing or maybe it's beginning again. I want a new beginning.

"I'm buying a peregrine," I offer. I've been pondering the possibilities of a new falconry bird for days. I say this like I've made up my mind. In fact, hearing myself speak the words, I know I have. "And no, I'm not trying to prove anything," I interject before she can respond.

"I wasn't going to say that," she says. My mom knows that even though I've been a professional bird trainer for six years, and a falconer longer than that, I've never flown a peregrine. I wasn't allowed to fly the show peregrines and couldn't really afford one of my own. Peregrines aren't just expensive, they're easy to lose and hard to train. Really, there's much to prove.

I spent the last season flying a merlin, a tiny bird-hunting falcon. I caught a lot of sparrows with her, but the doves I tried so hard to help her catch eluded us. I want to hunt doves in the desert where I live. I tell my mom that the best way to do this is with a small peregrine, a male. I've found one too; a tiercel peregrine bred just an hour and a half away. It's a Cassini/Anatum, a cross between a North American and South American sub-species that I believe will make for a good-natured bird that can tolerate the heat. I say that I want to hunt dove with a peregrine, but I know it's more than this. It means so much more than this. I'm just not sure how to explain it, not even to myself.

"What does Adam think?" My mom asks this innocently, but I can't help but take a gulp of wine before I answer.

"I don't know. I didn't ask his permission." I meant to answer with a laugh, but my reply sounds sharp. Adam and I have been dating just over six months. He's the only falconer

I've ever dated and though we're the same age, he's got seven more years on his falconry license than me. However, he's never flown a peregrine either and in many ways I have just as much experience as he does. We don't tell each other how to fly our birds.

"Are the two of you fighting?" Mom asks this with a sigh. "I know you're set in your ways, but Adam seems like the right one. I know you love him."

I don't answer her, because I do love him and wonder if she is right. Sometimes I'm too hard on my boyfriends. I don't like to bend. Still, I swore I would never date a falconer and I certainly bent that personal rule.

Adam and I meet every other weekend to hunt our birds alone or with friends during the day. There's nearly a three-hour drive between us, between the desert and the beach, and it's usually me that makes the drive. I tell myself it's an easier drive for me and that there are more places for us to hunt near the beach. I enjoy hunting with Adam, but it's the nights that I love.

When it's too dark to fly, we tie our birds on inside perches, warm safe places to sleep, and we make love until the tangle of our bodies doesn't seem to be saying enough. Then we swap falconry tales until we're too tired to remember which of the stories are our own and in our haze recount one another's personal legends in slurred descriptions and shared language. Like the last priest and priestess of a beautifully archaic religion, we whisper about God in a miracle hunt, in a surprise victory stolen from the last moments of daylight or clasped in the talons of weary hawk. We are certain we've seen moments like no one else.

"I don't know what Adam will think," I tell my mom. I say this, but when I get off the phone, if I'm not too drunk, or maybe even if I am, I'll call him and tell him and I know what he'll think. He'll think I'm crazy and beautiful.

My mom and I talk too long into the night for me to call Adam. We stop laboring over the past; instead imagining the possibilities of a peregrine and my mom's work as a quilt designer, treating both as discussions of art. She explains the "flying geese" quilt that she is working on, describing the design and colors while I try to imagine. I don't understand quilting any more than she understands falconry, but I love the idea of birds migrating across cloth. Later in my sleep I dream of snippets of floating fabric and wake wondering if my mother dreamt of falcons.

Adam isn't surprised when I call the next day and ask if he will come with me to pick up my new peregrine. I pretend like his nonchalance doesn't bother me. The last time we talked I hadn't liked the conversation and had suggested I might need a "time out" from dating. He had said, "I'd rather you didn't, but do what you have to."

That was a week ago and I had imagined he might be wondering by now just how angry I was, but his tone is of a man who was expecting a phone call at any moment. Now I'm wondering if I was angry enough to buy a peregrine, but should have made better use of my ire. Maybe I'm just trying to prove that life will go on without him, even if he does decide to take a job editing pornography in the Valley. If I am, I might only be proving it to myself.

Adam is a talented videographer and editor and desperately needs the money, but I can't be one person removed from that industry. I know it from its periphery, but from close enough to know it well. It's not the product that bothers me. It's the drugs, the aching esteem of everyone involved and the spiral down that's too strong to resist. I'm not afraid for him. I'm afraid for myself and he's not listening.

So I'm not going to say, "This peregrine could replace you. And even though it would break my heart, it would be over with us if you took that job." There is no point in saying it. I communicate with actions and will instead, the same way we communicate with our birds. He knows what I'm saying.

"Do you know Tom Austin?" Adam doesn't let the conversation lull. He pretends we're speaking from an uninterrupted relationship. He also knows how to derail me with a question.

"I met him once. It wasn't pleasant," I answer, understanding that Adam just got the upper hand. I'm buying my bird from Tom Austin and have to go to his house to pick it up. Tom is notorious. Many admire his high-flying, hard-hitting birds. Many also don't care for the man himself. Now in his fifties, he's spent three decades earning his reputation for a volatile temper and a sharp tongue. I want Adam to come for support and Adam knows it. "You went out and shot falconry footage at his place last year, didn't you?" I ask this because I know he did and that the Austins liked him. Jenna Austin told me as much on the phone when I arranged to buy the falcon.

"Tom's all right." Adam doesn't sound committed. He's waiting for me to admit I'm nervous and need him to go with me.

"So you'll go?" I ask, but am answered with silence. "Tom would probably be more likely to talk to you. You know how it is." I'm irritated by this fact and Adam still isn't answering me. "Adam, it's my *first* peregrine." A long silence follows and I stare at my hiking boots.

"It would be good to see Tom again." Adam finally agrees, knowing I need him and more than that, knowing I can't stand to buy my first peregrine and not have him there with me. We don't speak about the possibilities of him working in adult entertainment. Instead we set a time to meet at my place and talk about how amazing a peregrine will be and how great it will be to see each other again.

I don't want to know who won the battle of wills over how Adam will make better money, so I don't wonder. Instead I remember a weekend that we spent in Palm Desert staying at what amounted to a Southwestern-style palace in the Bighorn Country Club. I was house-sitting while the owners were in Africa and they had told me to be sure to bring my boyfriend out for a weekend. So I had.

Adam and I had flown his red-tailed hawk all afternoon on a Saturday, hunting jackrabbits in a dry river bottom. We had come back to our palace, both of us dusted with glinting sand, smelling of sage and the wild sand verbena I had tucked behind my ear. We sat up all night drinking Tres Generaciones tequila by the brick fire pit outside, marveling at the heady change in the air when a surprise thunderstorm moved in and away.

In the morning when he left I had meant to give him a quick kiss and run back inside. I was still giddy with our laughter and lack of sleep, but when I started to turn away, he pulled me back, no longer laughing and cupped my face in his hands. With the edge of his palms beneath my chin and his fingers at my temples, he leaned in and kissed me so slowly and deliberately that my knees buckled and I had to lace my fingers behind his neck to steady myself. When he pulled away, he paused to look in my eyes to make sure I understood, and then as if he wasn't sure I had, he said, "I love you." I repeated the words automatically and stood stunned as he left, staring after his truck long after there was nothing left to see. I knew

I would spend the rest of my life comparing kisses to that one, comparing relationships to a single kiss.

Pressing my fingers to my lips, I remember it again and think that a moment like that should be enough of a promise to save any relationship. Honestly, I can't wait to see him. I wonder though, is love enough or am I just my mother's daughter?

Chapter Two

Some Birds Weren't Meant to Be Trapped

New falconry birds merit a celebration similar to bringing home a new puppy or buying a fast car. Falconers love to be on hand the moment someone lifts a new falcon on their glove for the first time. We want to examine markings, "kick the tires," offer prophetic announcements about the bird's possibilities, but above all else, drench ourselves in the excitement of a new falconry season's potential, even if only vicariously.

Adam is excited about picking up a new bird as well. We laugh and tell trapping stories in his gold Tacoma on the way to Temecula to pick up my bird. Some birds are trapped and kept for merely a season. I describe my first hawk and how we couldn't trap the one I wanted, the one every apprentice that year wanted. Falconers are only allowed a red-tailed hawk or a kestrel in their first two years, and because kestrels are too small to catch more than mice and sparrows, most of us fly red-tails.

The apprentices all start scouting when trapping season starts on October first. What hawk you trap becomes a status symbol. A big hawk or a hawk with unique coloration situates your ranking as an apprentice, at least the first year. Few people other than apprentices fly red-tails and those flying red-tailed hawks with a first-year bird's brown tail are likely a first-year falconer. We are all looking for some way to stand out.

I, too, agonized over my first bird as an apprentice. It had taken over a year to convince a falconer to sponsor me, a requirement of being an apprentice. And still, the falconers humored me rather than taking me seriously. I wanted a bird like no other. I wanted a reason to be regarded with interest. I was too new to realize that the hawk on my glove wouldn't make me a falconer. It would ultimately be the way that hawk hunted and her decision to continually return. I didn't know this. So I desperately wanted that dark hawk that haunted the edges of the car dealership on Jurupa Avenue.

Once I had passed the falconry test, built a "mews" for a hawk to live in and had paid for my licensing, my sponsor's signature on the paper work, I waited patiently for the first day of trapping season. I would use a baited trap dressed with slip-knots that would catch the hawk's toes when she tried to grab at the prey. I had read falconry books in elementary school, mining the meager resources in the local library. I knew this trap from these old books and could picture the messy line drawings of bal-chatri traps.

What my friends called a "BC" I remembered from one of these reference books. It was a trap made of hardware cloth which was bent into a dome and attached to a wooden platform, lengths of monofilament tied one by one until they made a blanket of tiny clear nooses on the metal.

Every falconer has a trick to making their own trap. Every falconer has the best way. I learned this on trapping day when we all gathered at dawn. I discovered that although the bird was for me, the trapping was actually a competition between the men. Jay, Will, Simon, and Henley all had their own fool-proof methods. One painted the metal so that it wouldn't shine. Another added a base made of rebar so that the metal didn't flip when tossed like a Frisbee from a moving truck. Everyone had a different idea of the sort of bait that should go inside the trap. A white mouse, a wild mouse, a gerbil, a hamster, and although none would be harmed, surely one was better than the other to hear the falconers talk.

However, no matter how perfect your BC, the hawk has to be hungry enough to bother investigating the strange contraption. The surprisingly dark bird that we all wanted to catch had a full crop of food protruding below her chin the first morning we went trapping. That didn't stop us from trying. She was too exquisite to ignore, a chocolate-feathered bird amongst the normally pale hawks. We laid out three traps one by one, but all she would give them was a glance and then she flew to another pole as if bothered. My trapping crew became bored and we searched for another bird.

We drove for an hour looking for hawks perched on the pole line, joking back and forth on channel ten of the CB radio. "Hey, Rebecca, how about that melanistic red-tail? Do you want it?" Jay teased over the CB, drawing our attention to a golden eagle perched high above the road.

I hadn't seen many eagles and wished that we could. I would have loved to hold her in my hands for a moment just to feel her strength explode between my palms when I set her back to the air. However, we would all lose our license trapping eagles if a warden caught us. "That thing would fly off with your BC," replied Will, and we kept driving.

We all saw the pale female at the same time, made the same assessment. She was in a good spot to lay a trap away from traffic and definitely a first-year bird. We weren't allowed to take adults. We trapped passage birds on their first migration, not haggards. This made her a good choice.

Will drove by slowly and I tossed the BC beneath her. We parked down the street, all of us watching with binoculars except for me. I had a video camera trained on the trap. I watched her lean tentatively closer with the jerky hesitance of a hunting reptile. There was no change in her carriage to mark her decision. She snapped a foot at the mouse inside with a smooth motion that made me start behind the camera. She gave in to her own panic when her foot wouldn't come away from the wire and she found she was trapped. Wings stretched wide and battling for her freedom, she was fierce, dangerous, and looked as big as an eagle to me. That's all the video I got. The rest is shaky shots of pavement as I'm running for my prize.

"What did she weigh?" Adam asks. This is what we always ask.

"She weighed 1030 grams," I say "and flew at around nine hundred." It's odd that I can't remember my best friend's birthday after fifteen years, but I can still remember my first hawk's weight. That's how important that hawk becomes, how important falconry becomes.

The hawk is wrapped up like a tamale, Velcro around her legs, pantyhose holding her wings against her. I've spent all day trapping. I'm exhausted and know that I need to get this bird back to the mews I've built for her, but I just have to make one side trip.

My grandfather has the garage door open. He's sawing wood, building towel racks or maybe napkin holders. He lives alone now, but always has a new project to keep him occupied. He turns off the saw and comes out to greet me.

"I've trapped my hawk," I say to him, and he looks into my truck, puzzled. Perhaps he expects it to be loose in the cab. I laugh at the idea and I hold her up to show him.

"What in God's name have you done to it?" He asks.

"She's okay. I'll undo her when I get home."

"Not very big. I thought it would be bigger," he sniffs.

"Big enough to catch rabbits," I say, but I'm a little disappointed until I realize he's teasing me. All my life he's been teasing me and I fall for it every time.

"I would really like to see that," he says and smiles. I would really like him to see it as well, but I don't say it. I give him a kiss and tell him that I have to get going.

"You took the first one you trapped then? Not very patient," Adam says.

"They're all about the same," I say, but wonder if I wasn't just a little desperate.

"So did anyone get that dark bird?" Adam asks. Someone did. Another apprentice was more determined than I was or perhaps less anxious to have a hawk in hand. Several weeks later he finally trapped the melanistic hawk.

"How did he trap it?" Adam asks with a smile on his face that makes me reluctant to answer him. I could have trapped that hawk if someone had told me how.

"He did a dig in," I say, as if I couldn't be bothered with such a thing myself.

"Smart," Adam says with an admiration that I can't completely dismiss. A dig-in requires shoveling out a hole big enough to climb into. The falconer gets in and covers himself with branches and leaves, his hands held up just high enough to hold some tasty morsel, but not reveal what's holding the other end. When the hawk comes down to this less suspicious meal, the trapper grabs her by the legs. It takes effort, patience, and faith in your ability to grab the business end of a hawk.

"She wasn't worth it," I note with only a tinge of jealousy, because it's true. It took weeks to get the well-fed hawk hungry enough to take food from the man who had wrenched her from the wild and then even once she got going, the bird was always unpredictable. I had thought to myself that she had understood we were all trying to catch her and was too proud to get over the deceitful way she was captured. Some birds weren't meant to be trapped.

"You had a good bird your first year. I remember, Sadie, right?" Adam says. He rubs at the blonde stubble on his chin, smiles at me and then reaches for a Marlboro. I feel my cheeks warm and turn to look away, smiling out the passenger-side window because we didn't know one another very well then and because she *was* an excellent hawk. I just wish I had taken my grandfather hunting with her when I had the chance. I wish he could come with us to see this new peregrine.

CHAPTER THREE

Defining a Mentor

Tom Austin looks exactly the same as when I first saw him seven years before and I suck air between my teeth, on edge and too afraid of what I might say wrong to speak. He is tall and lean, at least six feet, four inches, and he lumbers toward the truck, white hair still wild despite being forced beneath a baseball cap. It might be the dark eyebrows contrasting with the wizard shock of hair and close-cut beard, but his expression is intense and doesn't change. He looks like he's about to say something combative.

"Hey," is all he says as we step out of the truck in his driveway. Yet he seems to be saying enough. The last time I saw him he was threatening to slash tires on the vehicles of a couple guys who were hunting on his turf. Ponds were getting hard to come by and the land wars had just started. I had only been there to glimpse a falcon flying. I wasn't really a part of the crew. I can't imagine that he would remember me. At least this is what I'm hoping as he turns to me after greeting Adam.

"Have we met before?" he asks pleasantly enough, for him.

"I've been around for a while. You've probably seen me at a meet," I answer. Adam is smiling at his feet.

"So you want to buy this falcon?"

"I only have eight hundred dollars." I meet his eyes.

"The bird is a thousand. Pay me what you can now, the rest later. But if you lose him, you still owe me."

"Okay," I say, because that's all there is to say. There was never room for negotiating.

"You ever fly a peregrine before?"

"No," I say.

He shakes his head and beckons for me to follow.

The falcon is in the weathering yard, an enclosed area where we keep them during the day to get sun and bathe. They are tied to their perches so that they don't hang from wires and break their precious feathers and so constant flight doesn't make them wild once more. Tom points to the one that is mine and I crouch to look across the small yard and into his face.

The full cap of feathers painting his head is so black that I can barely make out his dark eyes darting from my face to my hands. He is preparing to fly from me as if he could break the bond of the anklets, jesses, and swivel that bind him on a perch. His long pale toes lay light on the green Astroturf ready to rise at any moment. He is only a week away from his parents, thrust into a world of nimble human fingers and strange pale eyes that visibly changes with the light. I marvel at the strength of the slender wings that beat two strokes of warning into the air, bothering strands of my hair, making me take a slow step back.

We are something new to one another, but recognize each other in our careful inventory of features. The falcon bows his head as I straighten my shoulders and raise my chin. We are adversaries, already matching wills.

"His mom is Anatum and his father is Cassini," Tom explains and tells me why he likes the Cassini subspecies. He likes their wingbeat and their speed. He likes that they are good-natured but aggressive in the field. "They're dark birds and this one had great coloring. He'll be a great duck hawk if that's what you want."

I'm listening to Tom, but I find myself imagining another falcon. I'm trying to remember that long-ago falcon and how much it looked like this one.

The falcon shifts her weight precariously; right foot to left and the television antennae on the roof where she is perched wobbles with the unexpected weight. My grandmother is probably inside, smacking the TV, trying to smooth the lines from the irritated reception, unaware of what is going on outside. My grandfather is pointing at the dark falcon when I hear the enticing whisper of bells shifting along with the falcon's weight.

"She's a falconry bird. Hear the bells? Look at the leather straps on her legs. They're called 'jesses,'" my grandfather explains. I only nod. I've been living with him for four years and he is constantly pointing and teaching like this and I'm constantly intrigued.

The falcon is an amalgamation of perfect symmetry, dangerous curves, and dark eyes. I assume my grandfather is right when he refers to her as she. Her black gaze seems impenetrable, yet still kind and forgiving. Above her stare, her brow is so heavy that I imagine every thought is complicated, deep. She is royalty.

"She belongs to someone?" I think of loss and how desperately I would miss her had I lost her. I don't understand falconry, jesses, or falcons, but I'm captivated. She knows we are standing beneath her and she's indifferent. I'm only eight, but I do understand that her indifference makes us kin.

I'm not entirely listening when my grandfather explains that someone hunts ducks with this gorgeous bird. Instead, I'm imagin-

ing walking in her shadow, having a bond so inseparable that even flight can't sever it. I picture a bird on my glove like the drawings I've seen in my animal encyclopedia under "peregrine falcon."

I see a falcon coming back from an endless sky and this is all I'm envisioning as my grandfather carefully explains falconry in California and why a falcon might be on our roof right here in the suburbs of Riverside.

I stop pretending to listen when the falcon begins to row her wings and stare at the sky. Her bells are ringing out her wingbeat and my heart is doubling the chime. She's leaving. I haven't convinced her of what our friendship might be worth and she's already discarded me for the horizon. Doesn't my grandfather see?

His litany fades into silence when her wings grab the sky and she pulls herself away. He watches her go, accepting her flight as enough of a goodbye and the lecture as done, but I stay outside watching the sky for hours.

Tom grabs a falconry glove hanging from a hook and hands it to me along with a quail breast he has brought from the kitchen. "Pick him up. He'll start eating when he gets on the glove."

I want to pick him up, but wince. The falcon doesn't know me. I know he's going to bate, jump from the glove and hang upside down. Falcons can break feathers this way, inhibiting their ability to maneuver in the air. Worse if hanging long enough, the opposite rush of blood can kill them. Mostly though, I just don't want to watch him trying to get away from me and I don't want Tom to see it either.

It's my job to make the falcon's world a place where he doesn't feel constrained by two bits of leather, but instead wears his jesses, the strips of leather that hang from his legs, like his feathers. I want to train falconry birds who never feel the need to jump and hang themselves. A comfortable falcon preens his equipment into place and is even more confident on the glove of his falconer than his perch. It will be a long road to get this falcon to that place.

I scoop the falcon up quickly and when he's upright on my glove he glares at me directly. I look away, pretending I'm not a predator, pretending Tom isn't watching me like a hawk as well. I know this is a test of basic falconry. I am demonstrating that I can read a raptor, put him at ease even though something deep inside of him is whispering that I am dangerous, that I am not to be trusted.

Eyes still downcast, I slowly move my right hand so that I can tap the food tucked in the glove below the falcon gently with my fingers. The movement gets his attention and he bows his head cautiously several times, not so sure he wants to expose the back of his head to me. I'm holding my breath, still only watching from the corner of my eyes. Then at last with one more angry glare he settles in to eat a cautious meal.

Tom shows no signs that I've proven myself in any way. He shrugs and walks away while the falcon works at his meal, leaving me to warily take in the bird that as of tomorrow will become my every morning's priority.

The peregrine is so light on my glove. We weigh them in grams, because ounces aren't precise enough to judge the incremental changes in their airy bodies. He is slightly smaller than a crow, less than half the weight of most ducks, and I can't imagine him catching one. In fact, I've never seen a falcon catch a duck anywhere but in my imagination. It doesn't matter if he can catch ducks or not. I've bought him to hunt desert doves.

He has the plumage of a first-year bird, brown and buff spotted chest, black back. Next year, after he's molted each feather, replacing them one by one in the summer's heat, he will have a blue back and a peach colored chest. He'll wear those adult colors no matter how many more molts he lives through, a success we mark as intermewed. Falconers name their bird's age by saying they are twice, three times, or how many times intermewed. His juvenile plumage is to be admired and remembered. It only lasts a year.

When Tom returns I ask, "How soon should I get him in the air?"

"As soon as you can. As soon as he's solid on the lure. Maybe two weeks. You've got a lure right?"

"I'll make one tonight." I should already have a lure, the leather pouch we use to entice a falcon out of the air, and I can't believe I haven't thought of this. Gauging Tom's expression he knows I haven't thought through my training plan. Adam isn't impressed either.

"Feed him on the lure as soon as he's comfortable eating on your glove," Tom makes this a command.

"But just garnish it the first few times," I say thinking of a Lanner falcon I worked in a show. Whether there was food on the lure or not, this falcon would spread his tail and wings over the pouch, so rabid to protect it that the fragile feathers wore and broke at the ends until he had half a tail and frayed wings. I thought it was better to eat on the glove.

"You always garnish the lure," Tom orders. I look at Adam, but he's already turning away, knowing I'm going to argue.

"I don't agree." I watch Tom's dark eyebrows twitch and begin to state my case. He interrupts me.

"You've never flown a falcon before."

"That's not the point," I say. I try to explain the Lanner falcon and understand Tom's reasoning. Some falconers would argue that the only thing worse than a dead falcon is one with broken feathers.

"Just try it my way."

"I'm just trying to understand your way," I say.

"You're arguing," he says.

"I'm just getting you to articulate your reasoning," I say carefully. He raises his eyebrows and tries explaining in a new metaphor.

I'm feeling like I understand when I leave, even though Tom is watching me with permanently hoisted eyebrows. Admittedly, Tom makes me nervous, but I feel like the gorgeous dark falcon on my fist is worth the tense discussion.

"Call me," Tom says as a way of goodbye. "I hate it when guys take my birds and don't call."

"What are you going to name him?" Adam asks when we are safely down the driveway in his truck. He rolls down his window so the cigarette he's lighting doesn't waft even a tendril of smoke in the direction of the falcon on my glove.

"Anakin," I say.

"Anakin, like Skywalker?"

"If I'm going over to the dark side, who better to go with?" I say. Although, what I'm thinking is that Tom Austin looks a bit like Obi Wan Kenobi.

CHAPTER FOUR

Peregrine Beginnings

Falconry is a religion, a way of thinking, a means of experiencing life. True falconers are compassionate, clear-eyed straightshooters. We've touched nature's senseless violence, clung to her stray miracles, and this alters our beliefs. It is a religion for which we are often persecuted. And at the center of falconry is a holy war for the peregrine.

Fifty years ago peregrines were considered vermin to be shot on sight. Many states had bounties that made sighting the gun on narrow wings profitable. Hawks and falcons were thieves that robbed humans of fine game, fattened chickens and lofted pigeons. There were few groups of people who valued the raptor. Yet the falconers valued them more than anyone. To the falconers there was nothing more perfect than a peregrine. Then the sea change came.

In the years before I was born falconry was nearly eradicated for the sake of the peregrine. The cosmopolitan falcon had remained a steadfast beloved to the falconer for more than three thousand years, but during the years of my childhood these birds nearly disappeared from North America. The falconers were just as mystified as the conservationists and then horrified when the blame was placed on their sport, on the few that loved them the most. Falconers were named nest-robbing soulless pirates.

The North American Falconers Association formed a committee "for the preservation of falconry" and waged a war for their rights. The falconers saved their art, keeping it legal, but lost the right to trap a peregrine. In order to preserve the privilege to hunt with raptors, we forfeited the wild take of *Falco peregrinus*.

Birds were no longer trapped on the beach to fly a single season and released on the migration. Eyasses were no longer tenderly tucked in a jacket pocket to be rappelled down the sheer face of cliff eyeries. Yet the falconers were determined. If they couldn't borrow them from the wild then they would breed them. And the falconers succeeded where the scientists did not. I didn't know it when I was eight years old, but the falcon on my roof was a miracle of desire.

Then the peregrine began to resurge as a wild population and burgeon as a captive-bred resource. When I was in high school the long-wingers, falconers who preferred the flights of the long-winged falcons, had their choice of flighted companions from many different breeding projects even if they weren't allowed to borrow them from the wild. As the captive-bred peregrine became more accessible, surprisingly the war resurged as well.

Scientists didn't believe that falconers could be successful breeding the falcons when others had failed. Surely, the falconers were laundering wild birds through fake breeding projects that couldn't possibly be producing young.

Across the United States Fish and Wildlife Agents knocked on the doors of sixty falconers. Search warrants in hand they tore through homes, mishandled birds, interrogated falconers, and confiscated their falcons. Described as "clumsy, clueless, ham-fisted, jack-booted storm troopers" they turned the falconry community upside down and heralded the beginning of Operation Falcon.

Some of the falcons confiscated were returned after lengthy, arduous, and expensive court battles. Others perished in the hands of the agency. Our government was convinced that falconers must be passing off wild birds as captive-bred young in their breeding projects despite the lack of proof. Tried in the media, we were all dubbed international falcon smugglers.

There was little truth to the accusations. In fact, the trial revealed that the main perpetrator was an undercover agent supplied with illegal birds by the government. He had been paid to set about entrapping whomever he could snare. Again the falconers fought for their rights, for the sake of their love of the peregrine. Again they won, but the damage was done. Federal agents, state authorities, and worse, the public had tried the falconers in the media and proclaimed them wildlife criminals.

The peregrine is off the endangered list. Young wild birds are now abundant and pester our trained falcons in the field. We long for the short-term company of a truly wild peregrine but wonder if we'll ever be allowed to trap them again. It's doubtful.

Driving home in silence, Adam somewhere in his own head, I think about how the falcon on my fist is the fruit of several bitter wars, his breeding the result of passion pushing science. Had the falconers given up, had either of those battles swung the other way there would be no license for my religion and I wouldn't have a peregrine.

When I was an apprentice, you could not put a captive-bred peregrine on your license, possess it legally, unless you were a master, a falconer with five years of experience. I've been a master falconer for some time now, but have never had a peregrine. I have a lot of excuses why. Peel those excuses away and I'm just afraid, afraid to fail, but this year I'm flying a peregrine anyway.

In February I turned thirty-two. There's nothing monumental about the number except that not long after my birthday I woke one morning with a memory that made it something more.

I'm seventeen and someone reads my palm. I can't see her face, just long dark hair, frizzing about her cheekbones, but I can hear the even tone of her proclamation. She says, "You will live to be thirty-two." Her voice is scratchy, unnaturally throaty.

She traces a line at the center of my hand that leads between my thumb and forefinger as if she is reading. She doesn't laugh or even smile, just traces a few more lines and drops my hand.

I can't even imagine living another fifteen years, so I shrug it off and turn away without looking back. I mean to forget it. I don't believe in the foretelling of death. No reputable fortuneteller would say such a thing, even a novice. It's against the rules.

Somehow, though, this girl had planted the thought and it reverberated like a ringing alarm when it was time to recall it, when somehow I found myself thirty-two. I keep bringing the memory back, trying to make the girl lift her face so that I can see it, bring out the details so that I can remember where we were, but I can't draw out more.

I know the lines of my hands now. I've studied them carefully, these etchings I was born with versus the white lines I once foolishly carved on my wrist. I don't know which is more of a portent, features or scars. Still, the lifeline that surrounds my thumb looks endless and strong. It is crosshatched over and over at its beginning stretch, a sign of hardship and stress. It smooths out in what's sure to mark my thirties and that has always left me hopeful for the future.

Madame Christine read my palm five years ago from a room in her doublewide at the edge of the Florida swamp. I had stopped on a whim, twenty dollars in my pocket, half my grocery money for the week. The bird show at Disney's Animal Kingdom didn't pay well, but I was hoping for a bright future. Madame Christine told me I was born under lucky numbers, but that I just hadn't gotten the luck yet. She promised it was coming and said I was going to live to be eighty-three. I asked her how she knew and she pointed to the left on my palm and said, "Right here," but I didn't see it.

I don't believe I'm going to die, but all the same, this year has become a big "What if?" What if this is it? I wanted to see more than thirty-two. More than that, I didn't want to waste this year. What if I never have another chance to fly a falcon?

I think about how the lines on my palms meet to form an "M" scrawled much like a child crayoning birds in the sky above stick figures, wonder if a life with birds was always in my future. Birthright or self-infliction, the falcon is the future I want.

"Why haven't you ever flown a peregrine?" I ask Adam. He shrugs.

"You've got plenty of places to hunt ducks," I say, wondering why someone who has flown birds for seventeen years would choose never to fly a falcon. He has access to much better terrain for flying long-wings than I do.

"I would rather fly a goshawk," he says without looking at the peregrine on my glove. "Besides, I've seen plenty of guys fly falcons. I've had my fill."

I run my finger over the falcon's longest toe, then press my fingertip to the point of the talon until the sharpness of it stings. It's fragile and powerful, a perfect contradiction. The bones so narrow, I could snap them between two fingers, but the strength of his piercing grip could draw blood from my bare skin in an instant. I can't imagine how you could ever get your fill.

"I hope you'll come watch this guy fly anyway."

"Get him in the air and we'll see," Adam says.

CHAPTER FIVE

To Tame a Peregrine

It isn't hard to wake at dawn when you can hear the stirrings of a falcon outside of your room. I lie in bed a moment, eyes closed and smiling. I had zip-tied a bell on the screen perch so that I can hear the falcon adjust, know if he bates, note if he gets back up. As the sun starts to light the room, the bell rings faintly, responding to the gentle vibrations of the falcon scratching his head. I listen just a little longer, knowing that my sudden appearance will cause him to tighten his feathers and think about flight. I hear him rouse, a hum of feathers that have all been lifted from the body and shaken down into place. My flannel sheets are too warm and I envy his feathers, warmth that can be adjusted precisely, individual muscles raising each shaft, allowing air to cool between skin and down. Then my African grey parrot calls, "Coffee?" in a believable intonation of my voice and the bell silences, the spell broken.

It's June and this is the low desert, one hundred degrees at midnight, no matter how dark the night or how many scorched acres are converted to lush lawn. The only time it's comfortable outside is at dawn. I pad over to the falcon in my pajamas, a tank top and boxers. I slip on my falconry glove, double-layer elk skin, cut from a tracing of my hand and sewn to fit and protect the skin just past my wrist, but I still feel naked and exposed when the falcon glares at me. I have too much skin showing, too many fragile parts, but I step him up on my glove.

I tell myself he's just a falcon, a tiny thing despite his giant temperament. I've hefted eagles on this same fist and haven't lost any appendages. Even the first red-tail hawk I flew as an apprentice falconer was twice this peregrine's size, thick-toed and broad-beaked; she was far more dangerous near my soft eyes and brittle finger bones. This head full of reasoning does nothing to override the chill in my gut when the falcon meets my eyes. He knows he's stronger than me and I'm not going to change his mind. So I keep his jesses tight, his feet close the leather glove as I walk outside to tie him to a perch on the patio.

The falcon needs to get in the habit of eating at dawn, have an appetite when we would normally be flying. He needs to learn that meals come off the lure and then we'll begin training in earnest. Without a lure the only way to get a falcon back is through a sacrifice of live game. Raising pigeons for slaughter is hard on the soul and bad training besides. Sure, you could throw a pigeon or some other farm raised game into the wind, draw the falcon down from the sky with a fluttering meal, but that's not training; it's only a reminder of what a wild heart is unable to resist.

Back in the kitchen, I take the quail I thawed during the night and cut it in half down the center, a leg on each side. I bought five freezer bags full, each stuffed with twelve farm-raised quail, three rows of four, carefully lined up so the bags stack nicely next to the vegetables and the ice. No different than chicken or Cornish game hen really, except that they haven't been cleaned or dressed. I tell everyone that they serve Coturnix quail in fine restaurants, but my friends still jump when they reach for ice to put in their sangria. I've learned to be strategic about when I thaw quail. Nothing ruins a dinner party faster than the words, "Um, there's a dead bird in your sink."

I put half the quail in a sandwich bag and then in the bottom crisper drawer for later. I pour myself a cup of coffee and then grab the lure so that I can tie the other half of the quail on it.

I made the lure the night before with much flailing of stitches and no shortage of needle-prick fingertip blood. It's ugly, this thing that I've made to signal the falcon to come back to me. It's an oval pouch, stuffed with plastic grocery bags to fill it out, flaps of leather at each side that vaguely look like wings, two grommets punched in the center so that I can run a string through them and attach some tempting food and another string sewn in the top so that I can swing it. As I tie on the food I think it looks like a bulbous lump, a tiny flat football, but it will have to do. At least the quail looks palatable.

Although I've never tried cooking any of this quail I've bought for years to feed my meat-eating birds, I think that it looks delicious. Not delicious in the way a spoonful of ice cream melts into sugar and cream on the tongue, but in the way a can of tuna at the end of a day-long hike seems to reach to your marrow. The opened quail looks like sustenance, like life. When I toss the lure in front of the falcon and step back, he jumps on it, eyes huge and wings out. I don't move, but think to myself, *Gotcha.*

I'm five years old stretched as long as my body will allow, my belly to the grass. I've got a salt shaker balanced in my right hand in the tips of my fingers as far out as I can stretch my reach. The salt shaker is in danger of tumbling from my tiny grasp, but I will it to remain. I try not to move. If I drop the salt shaker, I'll have to start again.

The sparrows picking through the seed I have strewn in the lawn are letting me get a little closer every time and I think this is it. I've been working on this all afternoon.

I don't want to keep one, not really. I just want to be closer. It isn't enough to watch. I want to hold one, to examine its toes and tiny talons, to examine where its beak hinges shut, to feel its feathers in my palms. I'll let it go right away, I promise silently. Then, at last, they are close enough.

I tighten my grip on the shaker enough to hang on as I jolt the crystal canister and toss salt in their direction. At least three of the birds have their backs to me, which is perfect because I have to hit a tail.

Everything moves at once, flying salt, flapping sparrows, but I am certain I saw bits of salt bouncing from one bird's tail. I saw it. Yet, the bird still flies away. I sit up for a moment trying to understand what has happened, but I know what has happened. It didn't work. It isn't going to work. I begin to wail and run for the house, the salt shaker pressed to my chest.

"Why are you crying?" my grandmother turns and asks as I fumble with the screen door to get inside. She seems worried and I'm sure she'll understand.

"Granddad said if I sprinkled salt on their tails," I suck in a sob and continue, "I could catch one."

"Howard," my grandmother yelps and I think I can hear my grandfather chuckling in the living room. I cry harder.

I settle four feet from the falcon on the ground, legs crossed, sipping my coffee. The falcon pauses to stare at me in between quick bites. I watch him without looking straight at him, raise the cup to my lips, scratch an ankle. I make this a game, moving only until his body indicates I'm about to make him nervous. To win I need the falcon to eat with his wings tight against his body, tearing at his meal with relaxed dips of his beak, no interest in my motions. If I keep playing this game, eventually I'll be able to stroke his long thin toes while he eats from between my fingers without a flinch. I need him to believe that I will never rip anything from his feet, never take anything he hasn't given up willingly.

I rub my nose and freeze when his wings drop to cover his food protectively. Hand to nose I wait for him to relax again and think that this is going to be a long haul, but I hate birds with bad manners, birds that mantle and scream. A bird like that is the sure sign of bad falconry. More importantly, a bird like that is miserable.

I have friends that mantle when they eat, usually men from a large family of brothers. They eat with their arms protectively stretched around their dinner plates, their heads bowed, gulping down their food. I worry about them, if they ever think they get enough to eat and if they ever believe that anything truly belongs to them. It makes me want to slowly ease my fingers beneath their elbows until at last they relax with the certainty that I would never snatch a morsel from their plate. Their posture is the same as a raptor concealing its food in the wild, where bigger predators abound and meals are easily taken or killed over. My falcon could be robbed or ripped into a meal by a hungrier raptor, but I want him to learn that meals are safely eaten in my company no matter the dangers that loom above. Wish I could do the same for my friends.

Half of a quail is a small meal and the falcon finishes quickly, jumping off the lure on the ground and to his slightly higher perch. He rubs his beak side to side on the edge of the perch. It looks as though he's sharpening it, but he's only cleaning his beak, feaking. It's the motion of a raptor that feels well fed and comfortable on his perch. It makes me smile. Someday he might even feak on my glove. For now though, I'm satisfied with this morning's worth of progress. I scoop up the lure, leave the falcon to get a drink of water from his bath pan and go inside.

There will be a few more days of this and then I'll have to find a field where I can fly him. I'll quit garnishing the leather pouch, despite Tom Austin's admonitions, but will step him up on the glove for a meal once he's grabbed at the lure. He'll come to understand the lure is a cue—that grasping it, then catching it, results in a meal.

At some point I'll make a mistake reading him and he'll get distracted and fly off. One thing at a time, though. Tomorrow he'll jump for the lure the length of his leash. The next day I'll tie him to a line and urge him to fly to it from ten feet and then twenty. I'll double the distance every time he comes without hesitation, go slower if he isn't sure he wants to fly. He's got to be certain before I can be certain.

Watching him from the sliding glass window I wonder how the season will go. I've trained or helped train at least one hundred birds over the last eight years. I've flown birds for shows in Florida, Ohio, Texas, and Australia, as well as here at home. Free flight shows demand precision training and as much faith in yourself as in the birds you encourage to fly back to your hand. Still, falconry is different. Hunting with a bird is harder, more dangerous, the natural risk of being a raptor just part of the deal. When seventy-five percent of fledged raptors don't survive their first year, you have to know you're up against the odds. Nature doesn't make exceptions for falconry birds.

I turn away from the window, reminding myself that he doesn't belong to me, that nature can take him back any time she wants. In fact, the government can do the same. As far as U.S. Fish and Wildlife is concerned, that bird on my patio belongs to them. They can knock on my door and take him for any reason they see fit. No amount of begging, reasoning or billable hours to an attorney will make a difference. When the feds come you have to careful.

My mentors have taught me to treat game wardens and nature the same. Never volunteer information, never underestimate, but always be respectful. They are neither friends nor enemies, but dangerous just the same. Falconers should foresee every possible danger; keep their facilities, equipment and papers in order with every detail recorded either to document the whims of nature or to prove there are no whims to their falconry. The birds don't belong to us, but any one of us will tell you that in the end it doesn't make a difference. Nothing can take away the hours that we've already stolen in the field. This morning I woke to the sounds of a falcon stirring and shared his breakfast, gaining a tiny bit of his trust. That's mine to keep.

Christopher Robin has great friends. I know this because mom has been reading me Winnie-the-Pooh. *I close my eyes as she reads, "Once upon a time, a very long time ago now, about last Friday, Winnie-the-Pooh lived in a forest all by himself under the name of Sanders."*

I try to keep my eyes closed, but I open them and giggle when Pooh climbs the tree after the bees and breaks the branch. I don't want to go to sleep. I want my mom to stay perched at the edge of my bed, the dark crown of her head peeking over the spine of the stiff book, her voice sweet and sounding like a smile.

My room is small but stuffed with things for little girls. The miniature reading chair my grandparents gave me with its red and orange blocky armrests is my favorite, but there are plastic baubles, plush toys and books everywhere. There are many books, mostly golden books, some with crayon-scribbled pseudo-letters from my hopeful hand. The books are my favorite toys even though I'm not old enough to read.

I don't have to read now though because I can hear my mom's voice as I drift off into the sleep I am struggling against. I will hear it every time I open a book about Pooh. Her sing-song storytelling lull will be mine to keep along with the black and white photo on the bedside table. I will dust off the photo even after it is hidden in the drawer and recall her words years after she's gone.

A week later in the field, the falcon is tied to parachute cord, a long piece attached to the swivel that hangs from the leather straps, the jesses at his ankles. I secure a transmitter on his tail in case my creance of parachute cord fails, and so he can get used to the weight. I place him on a perch in the center of the yellowing soccer field and walk away, my back to him.

Forty feet away, I slip a squirming starling from my pocket and before I have a chance to think on it further, toss it in front of me. I need to know he understands, that he has no reason to balk at a live meal. There isn't a moment to wonder if the peregrine comprehends, he's already on his way and I'm occupied with managing the lines, stepping back, moving behind, avoiding a hitch or a tangle. Then it's over.

The falcon and I look at each other, both startled. Then he bows his head slightly over the bird in his feet, snaps the neck and looks back up. He allows me to meet his gaze, seeing deep into his falcon's eyes and I understand that I could keep this predator on a line forever, but he will never be my pet. Over that shared look our relationship changes just a bit, because suddenly, we both grasp an obvious truth. I am looking into the eyes of a wild peregrine. It's so soon, only ten days, but it's time to let him fly free.

CHAPTER SIX

Flying Off

On the phone with Adam I joke about keeping the falcon on a line forever, talk about risk reduction and protecting the things you love.

"Pet keeper," Adam says, and I cringe. It's the worst thing you can call a falconer, insinuating that they have forsaken what's wild, that they lack the skills or the courage to finesse a real bond.

"I'm flying him free tomorrow," I say, but not with confidence.

"It'll be fine," Adam says without much conviction and though I answer with agreement, it's not what I mean. I want to explain that it's something more than free flying, than risk taking, but I don't know how to explain.

It's dangerous to be bound to something that can break your heart. If Adams loves, then he must understand this. I think about the way his eyes go out of focus when he talks about his dad, like a man looking inward for ownership to fault lines and rifts between father and son. There's so much to lose and no good guarantees. I don't have the words, so I end the conversation instead. Adam doesn't notice I'm distracted when we get off the phone.

I watch as the peregrine runs feathers through his beak one by one, smoothing oil and dust through each layer above down. Barbules zip together. Quills straighten. All become the perfect clothing of well-groomed plumage.

This first peregrine is a wonder, the way all new falconry birds are a wonder. It's not that he's unique. It's just that other wild birds won't permit you to stare into their feathers while they smooth them into place, beak dipping to preening gland, their busy head oiling plumage into silk. This isn't trust, just acceptance of circumstance. He accepts me as an annoyance, but only because I haven't yet proven to be a predator.

I am so tired, but can't resist watching the falcon. I will him to glance away from the busy work of necessity and comfort. I wish he would meet my gaze. If only he would see my face and associate its image with the reassurance of settling in for the night. If only he would look at me, maybe I would feel like a known presence with features to seek from the sky. Then maybe I would worry less over the possibility of him flying away in the morning.

I'm four years old and I'm sitting on my father's bed. He's shoving his fresh laundry into his dresser. I'm focused on the pink pig perched on the chest of drawers. I've never been able to reach it and have always wanted to shake it. I know also that in the bottom drawer there's a bottle that lives in a blue velvet bag with yellow cursive writing. The bottle is dark and flat. It's never been opened so I don't know what is inside, but that doesn't matter because it's not the treasure of choice. It's that bag I want to own. I want to put things into it, forget about them and pull them out again. There are so many wonderful things that could be hidden in a soft meridian bag. I want it more than anything else that belongs to my father, but I've always been too afraid to ask. Now I only think on the bottle and the bag for a moment, because the question I have to ask is an even harder one.

My father pushes his socks into the dark reaches as if he were punishing something in the drawer. I know that if I wait I won't be able to ask this question that I need an answer to so badly. If I don't ask soon it will be like yesterday when I sat at the kitchen table, opening and shutting my mouth like a fish while he stared at me, waiting. The question was a rock in my chest, the weight of it pulling at the back of my tongue. When I reached for my milk to wash it down, I knocked over the green Tupperware cup and he sent me to my room. I can't chance that tonight. I take a deep breath.

"Where's Mommy?"

"She went to Arizona and she's never coming back."

I open my mouth, but again I'm a fish, my father staring the words back down into my throat. I want to ask why. I want to ask how she could leave me. I want to ask what I did. I can see in his eyes, though, that it must have been something even a daddy can't forgive so I get up off the bed and without being told, go to my room. Some questions just don't get answered.

I would hate to lose the falcon, wonder where he went and why. I stretch across the couch that sits next to the screen perch I built, flexing my toes beneath him, I catch his attention. He turns his head sideways, then upside down, feathers forgotten over the intrigue of a human foot. Four weeks away from his parents, he's never seen anything like it.

I wasn't there when Tom Austin pulled him from the chamber, the room where he lived with parents and sisters in seclusion and safety. Most falconers don't like to raise our birds from chicks. We want them to differentiate falcon from human, have the tiniest bit of mistrust. We love our falcons wild and hunting for themselves, not begging at our feet for a tidbit or wrestling food from our hands. We want them to learn to trust us, not depend on us. So we let them fledge in the chamber, feed them through a chute, never allow them to know that all their food and comfort comes from a creature free of feathers and connected to the earth.

When the falcon is sixty days old we introduce ourselves with a net. Falcons scream and bounce off the walls, while the falconers try to catch the young birds quickly, safely, and with as little stress as possible, but the stress is unavoidable. I don't like to think about this, a moment that must be pure terror. I don't like to imagine being caught up just as you're learning to fly and taken from everything you know. Falcons are not little people. I know better. A young peregrine quickly learns to accept almost everything, but I'm glad I wasn't there to see his face peering out from the folds of the net.

I'm four and my Raggedy Anne suitcase is stuffed with clothes, more clothes than when I normally visit my grandparents across the street. I don't think I've ever taken it to Pumpkin Land, my school, even though my grandmother has picked me up before. She's smiling at the teacher, the one who called my mother when my ears ached so badly that all I could do was cry. I think they ache now, but I understand that no one will be calling my mother. So I flip open the silver latches on the top of the suitcase with careful clicks that no one notices. When my grandmother beckons me to follow, I swing the suitcase forward and all of my clothes fall to the floor. They collide in a splash of colorful dresses and white panties, collecting in lost heaps. My grandmother sighs, already bothered although I'm not yet ensconced in my new bedroom. She stuffs the clothes back into my suitcase and I don't even wonder when I'll see my father again. I just follow behind, counting the steps to the green Impala waiting outside, waiting to drive me away to where I know I'll be staying for good. I know this, but I'll imagine a parent will come claim me any day.

The falcon is entranced with my toes, but it's not enough to make him trust me. Still, I can't help but laugh and wiggle some more. I'm memorizing him and imagining him climbing up through a cloudless sky, wondering how I'll find him. I don't have much practice and a high-flying falcon is so hard to see. His view of me will be just fine, but I'll have to convince him that he should come back. I'm not so sure I'll manage this. He's not bothered by me, but doesn't like me much. He hisses when I raise my hand and show him my glove, asking him politely to step up and come with me. He eventually climbs up, but it's always grudgingly and always with a squeeze of his talons and a defiant glare into my eyes. Some might tell me he's not ready, don't fly him free, but I don't subscribe to old falconry ideals and I believe we should work through this as equals.

A thousand years ago and more, there were no chamber-raised falcons. The science of breeding peregrines was developed in my lifetime to save the population dwindling in America, poisoned by DDT. Before breeding was a possibility most falconers trapped wild birds a little older than mine. They caught them up by tricking them into grabbing easy meals from traps, catching their long toes in man-made nooses. These falcons were already hunting, already wildly defiant, but couldn't resist what looked to be a hobbled starling, pigeon, or dove. They would, however, most certainly resist their captures.

Frederick II's falconry manual tells how one must seel a newly caught bird. With a hot needle and thread you carefully sew their eyelids closed, shutting out the light, robbing them of their greatest talent, sight. The bird is handled for sometime, weeks perhaps, before the stitching is slowly undone and the bird returns to a world that can be seen. The Arabs, bound to the ancient ways, still use this technique and I've heard that it works amazingly well. I don't doubt it. This is breaking. In modern psychology it's called "learned helplessness." This is where you crush an animal's desire to fight. Why is it that we believe broken things are tamed possessions? I could never close a bird's eyes to the world.

I'm nine years old and I still don't know why I live with my grandparents. I tell the kids at school my mother's dead. I say my father is just busy. I have no details, what else can I say? The few times I've been brave enough to ask small questions, hoping for tiny clues, my grandmother asks, "Are you writing a book?" How can I write a book? I have no story and I have no place in their house.

I'm not allowed to have my toys in the living room and have since given up on my grandparents playing games. I'm supposed to play quietly alone in my room. I'm not allowed in the kitchen unless I'm setting the table. Everything on my plate must be eaten, even if it's overcooked, tasteless, and the same meal four nights in a row. Then I'm to be in bed at eight o'clock, but I never fall asleep before midnight.

When I do fall asleep, I often wake screaming to a sound so loud in my ears that I can't hear my own voice. It is a thousand mosquitoes humming and I'm certain they will drain my blood or carry me away. My grandparents take turns and take their time coming in to my room, turning on the light and convincing me there's no giant buzzing insect. They can never hear the sound and when it fades away I can't go back to sleep. My grandfather sprays the ceiling corners with Raid, he moves me to the couch in the den, he wakes me up to interrupt my sleep, but nothing stops the sound from coming back, not even my own bedtime rituals. There is no way to rid myself of the buzz that fills the chasm of what hasn't been said, what I'm not allowed to know.

I still jump out of my skin when a mosquito buzzes by my head, even though the phantom sounds stopped when I was teenager. Even though I know it must have been some form of hallucination brought on by stress, brought on by inability to control my world. I believe in learned helplessness, but it's not without repercussion.

In California we don't seel our birds. In fact, it is illegal to trap a peregrine. However, before the peregrine was protected, before we had to save them from modern agriculture, we trapped beach birds. They were Tundra peregrines on their way to South America in their first migration. I heard that this was ultimate falconry. I've been told the beach birds would eat off the glove in the first twenty-four hours, tamed. The California coast falconers didn't seel their birds, they "waked" them.

In the sixties, on the beach in tents sealed tight against the night, the newly caught peregrines were kept up until dawn. Tanned and blonde, the falconers drank beer, told stories, and blew marijuana smoke in their peregrine's faces. The smoke would fill the tent, making the birds woozy with the laughter and the drugged air. They would become too tired and too confused to fight their new life of anklets and jesses bound to glove. Waking was a kinder form of breaking, but breaking all the same. You can't forge a relationship with learned helplessness, you can only force one and it will always be tenuous. There is always the possibility that the peregrine will rediscover the strength of his heart.

I should be sleeping. The falcon and I will get up before daybreak, five thirty in the morning. Still, I can't bring myself to turn out the lights while he's still putting his feathers into place. His dark eyes are eased into peaceful ovals. The droop of his pale eyelids are protecting the dark lens from the tickle and debris of feathers, but it looks like methodic rest to me. He'll be ready in the morning. I'll be ready in the morning. He will wear two transmitters with fresh batteries. I just put two nine-volts into the receiver. I've programmed my cell phone with the numbers of the closest falconers. If he flies away, I'll find him. I'll teach him to believe in me. I'll convince him to come back next time.

Now he tucks his head into the soft folds of his back, hoping for sleep, creating his own darkness. I can stare at him all night, but I know what I really need to do is go to bed. This is falconry, flying a bird free. I'm not a pet keeper. I'm not a traitor. We have a pact to move freely about the world together. The falcon just doesn't know this yet. The falcon still needs to learn my place as a hunting partner, as the canine that flushes the game, as the safe haven from larger predators. He needs to learn this with an unbroken spirit. He may not learn quickly enough. I may not be an adept teacher, but this is the next step in our relationship.

CHAPTER SEVEN

Lure Flying

I'm up before the parrots begin to stir and ask for their breakfast. The grey's head is still tucked in his back when I flip on the light to brew coffee. The falcon, however, looks as though he heard me break away from my dreams and has been staring into the darkness with anticipation. There's no wariness in response to my arrival. Instead, he shakes his feathers into place and begins to turn and pace on his perch. This is a good sign, a hungry falcon who understands the business at hand. Still, there's another hour before it's light enough to see into the western horizon. I want to be awake for this.

Out in the soccer field by the Lutheran church, the falcon launches off the perch toward the lure the instant I start swinging. I serve the lure, swinging it toward him, pull it, and watch him wing by me.

I would hold my breath if I didn't need it to yell for his attention and am surprised when he turns back just as I call to him. He flies past where he expects the line to slow him and turns with absolutely no grace. He looks more like a turkey vulture than a peregrine. Then wobbling, he pumps his wings as best he can back to the lure. I don't know what I was worried about. This bird couldn't fly across the street yet, let alone to Mexico. He doesn't have the strength. He knew he was free, though. I was six feet away, kneeling on the lure line, but he tried to tug it away twice before settling in to eat.

He's mantling just a little and I don't like that he tries to drag the lure. There's a good chance it's my mistakes that have caused this less-than-perfect behavior and I accept that. It's easy to accept when I can tell myself that *I free-flew my first peregrine on the lure and now I am bringing him home*. I glance at my watch as I put the falcon in the truck, figuring in three hours Adam will be making a pot of coffee. I hardly wait that long to call and tell him that I'm lure-flying a peregrine.

My first falconry bird was a red-tailed hawk named Sadie. She flew at 940 grams, which makes her twice as big as the peregrine, but with a more solid and compact build. Her flight was broad-winged and conservative. Speed and maneuverability come differently to a red-tailed hawk. On a normal day, the hawk manages best by finding a tall pole and waiting for something she can drop on, whether it is a falconer's lure or a cottontail rabbit. Anything will do and the less effort required the better. A red-tail launching herself off a falconer's glove is ponderous, a slow take off on a long runway. Her glory is in her strength.

In a stiff wind a red-tail can set her wings, hanging above a hillside without a twitch or tilt and manage a hover. She will hang there like a kite on a string, her brick-red train of tail feathers solidly fanned while she waits for an unsuspecting meal to make an appearance below her. Then she is all ground-slamming muscle, resilient feathers and bones matched with brute strength. When a red-tail falls on prey, she wins. The hawk is a heavyweight, looking for that knockout punch so that no more energy need be wasted. A peregrine is a light-weight, so fast and sharp-hitting that you hardly know you are about to go down.

This is what I've learned swinging the lure for the falcon this week. You don't lure-fly red-tails. They don't have the ability, let alone the desire. So I have very little experience and the falcon gets better at lure-flying faster than I can manage to get better at swinging. Most mornings he catches the leather pouch long before I mean to let him have it. If he hits the lure, he gets it and a meal follows. I tell myself that this is only fair, that all I have to depend on is clear communication. What is the use of chasing treasure if it will only be yanked away? Yet, the falcon takes the prize from my clumsy hands too soon in my opinion and there's nothing for me to do about it but practice.

I am a chubby ten-year-old covered with freckles and road rash. My grandmother shoves rosehip pills into my palm every morning and insists I rub my broken skin with vitamin E. She is certain that I will grow up scarred and unappealing and tells me as much each time she notices the proof of my clumsiness. I'm trying to learn to ride a full-sized bike without training wheels, but my balance always fails me. Today it wasn't my fault, though. That jerky dark-haired boy that just moved into the house at the end of the cul-de-sac threw a soccer ball against the spokes of my front wheel. I tumbled shrieking over the handlebars and slid across the asphalt.

"I'm going to have your grandfather put the training wheels back on," my grandmother says, furious when she sees the scrape across my cheek.

"I'm getting better at it. I won't fall again." I'm promising, but my grandmother walks away. I just need more practice. I've been trying for almost a year, but I'll learn. I don't want the wheels back on.

My friend Robin has been riding a bike without training wheels for two years now. I just want to be like all the rest of my friends. I want to ride my bike to elementary school. I want to buzz down the street, chasing the other neighborhood kids until the streetlights come on and I have to go home.

"Come here," my grandfather calls to me from the garage. I swallow against a tight feeling in my throat. The tiny wheels are probably already cinched on my bicycle again. "I have something for you."

He is standing next to a red bike half as high as the one I'm learning to ride on. It's small, but it doesn't have training wheels. "It's Tracy's old bike," he says and smiles. He's talking about a teenage neighbor, but I've never seen this bike. "We can borrow it for a little while." He motions for me to get on. "Not as far to fall."

Even now there's a stray bruise on my thigh and the fleshy underside of my arm. I can't account for them. I'm so wobbly and unaware of the solid objects around me that the sharp stab of an impending bruise is forgettable. So swinging a lure just out of reach of a falcon purported to dive at speeds up to 240 miles per hour is probably asking too much of my hand-eye coordination. Still, I learned to ride that little red bike and after that I got on my big blue Schwinn ten-speed and rode that too. I can learn to lure-fly a falcon

When I lure-fly, I anchor the string of the lure with my left hand and swing it with my right. The right hand controls the arc of the lure's swing, which follows the turn of your wrist. You swing the lure in broad circles at your side, shoot it out toward the approaching falcon, and then pull it away by sliding the string back with your left hand. Then with a pivot and a flourish, you turn to face the falcon and let him whip back around for another try.

The point of lure-flying is to exercise the falcon, but when you watch them twist in the air and stoop in an effort to outdo you, there's no doubt that most falcons adore the game. You shoot the lure out just in front of the falcon as he is coming toward you, timing the aim of your lure close enough that you see the falcon's feet reaching out to catch up the leather, and that is when you pull it out of his reach. My challenge is to be faster than the falcon, to be dexterous enough not to accidentally knock him out of the air and calm enough not to wrap the swinging lure around my own neck. It looks gorgeously simple, like a sensuous tango when demonstrated by a good falcon and a better falconer. I don't want to imagine what it looks like when I do it.

I can see the dance in my mind and believe in my heart that I can learn. You can knock a falcon senseless if you hit it with the lure, light as it is. Worse, if he catches it and in that moment you pull away, he might lose a talon and his ability to grasp prey. I have to get better at this. I remind myself that I'm still constantly bruised but then again, I have never stopped dreaming of flight.

Lure-flying a falcon isn't simple, but it isn't impossible for anyone, even me. Yet, I was told that it was. I wasn't allowed to fly the falcons when I was working at free-flight bird shows.

In Toledo, Ohio, I supervised a new show that was contracted for the summer at the zoo. I was responsible for all the training, for managing the staff, for working with the zoo management. Despite this level of responsibility, I was not allowed to fly the peregrines. Only Peter, a trainer two years my junior in the company was allowed to lure-fly the falcons in the show.

The Barbary would appear on the backdrop of the stage, pause to seek out his target and then dive down toward the audience. Twisting and sweeping inches over the crowd, Peter urged on the falcon swinging the lure from a raised platform. He flew so close, he ruffled hair. The audience gasped, screamed, applauded as McCloud, our best Barbary, gave them their own reason to love falcons.

My boss was an old-time falconer from California who believed that falcons were a sacred bird. I desperately wanted to fly one, but he wouldn't allow me to learn. So on Peter's days off there was no falcon in our show. I thought perhaps I was too clumsy, or perhaps inept in some other way too embarrassing to point out. Yet I trained other birds to catch grapes in their beaks, streak across the stage and fly breathlessly close to strangers. I know I was a good bird trainer, but a part of me still believes there must have been a reason I was denied the falcons. Surely it couldn't have been just because I was female. Yet this fear is partially why I've never put a peregrine on my license. So I remind myself that I once learned to ride a little red bike.

I make a target on a tree, scraping an "x" in the bark with a rock; imagine it's the falcon and focus. I swing the lure, aim and shoot, pivot, turn, and keep swinging. I do this until my shoulder aches and there is a blister on my forefinger from sliding the parachute cord as I manipulate the string out and back in. I tell myself that I will keep doing this until the ache and the blister fade into muscle memory and I don't just fly, but dance with falcons in my sleep.

"How's the lure-flying going?" Adam asks me on the phone. I rub my shoulder and tell him that it's going fine. The falcon seems to be coming along well. I don't mention that it's me who's struggling. "You're going to bring him out with you this weekend, right? Matt is going to fly his Barbary falcon too."

"Sure," I say, although I doubt I sound sure. The thought of flying the peregrine someplace new and having witnesses to my lure-flying ineptitude makes my heart pound. However, it's another piece of the training; flying in new terrain and taking risks. "I'll be there tomorrow night around seven," I tell Adam and wonder how we'll fit the screen perch in his tiny apartment instead of imagining the flight.

CHAPTER EIGHT

Getting Lost

When I pull the hood and let the falcon survey the new area from my glove, I'm thinking about the coffee that Adam said we didn't have time to stop for, hoping that our lure-flying session will be over soon. My breath forms faint clouds in the air between the falcon and me. It's colder here in Camarillo.

The falcon sits for a long time, watching the fleet of white-crowned sparrows and flycatchers darting through the air above us. He sits far longer than usual, but I tell myself that it's because we are in a new place and try not to think about Adam and Matt who are watching behind me. At last the peregrine takes off and heads to the west. I wait until he's turning and then pull out the lure and start swinging, but he doesn't come in. The falcon keeps climbing and doesn't seem to be looking at me. Then he starts to drift away and my heart beats a little faster. I notice Adam now at my left elbow and calmly ask, "What do you think?"

"I think you better get him down," he answers. *No kidding*, I think, but say nothing. I just swing the lure with a little more fervor, but it's not enough to get the falcon's attention. After a few more minutes he becomes an indistinguishable speck on the horizon. When I turn to go back to the truck to get the receiver, Adam already has it and hands me the little metal box with collapsed yagi antenna.

There is already tension between us. No one likes tracking birds. Friendships have ended over tracking sagas gone ugly. I concentrate on my receiver and taking deep breaths as I unfold the antenna, flip on the box and dial in the signal. I scan the direction I last saw the falcon with the receiver, watching the needle bounce on the face and pinpointing where the signal is strongest. Then I turn the receiver horizontal and vertical, determining which way the antenna on the transmitter might be hanging. That will tell me if he is in the air or has landed. Then I point out the falcon's direction to Adam. "He's still in the air and the signal is moving, but I guess we better go find him," I say, conceding to the fact: he isn't coming back, he's flown off.

"Let me see," Adam says and reaches to take the receiver from me. When I don't move or say anything he says, "What? I just want to see."

I want to tell him that I've probably tracked far more birds than him over the years I spent working flying things into new shows in strange places. I want to tell him that I'm perfectly capable of reading the receiver and he should get in the damn truck and drive me in the direction I just pointed. Instead, I hand him the receiver.

Adam swings the receiver in a replica of my same motions then grunts, turning back for the truck. He climbs in and I follow. Starting the truck, he waves goodbye to Matt, heading off in the direction where I had pointed. There's no time for socializing when a bird is heading for the hills. Matt understands and will expect us to call him when we get the falcon so that he knows what happened.

Rolling down his window Adam balances the receiver to get a signal. I think about asking for the receiver back, but if he wants to drive and track at the same time, let him. It would be much easier for me to manage the equipment, but I don't feel compelled to point that out. Instead I tell myself that at least no one was able to watch me lure-fly and scrutinize my skills. Then I tuck my hands back into my jacket again and wish I had some coffee. Adam should never have been so cavalier about getting me some later. We should have made plans as if the falcon might fly away. I don't know the bird well enough to know when his whims might overtake him. Sometimes the only way to find out when a bird is too hungry, too distracted, or far too focused is to make a mistake and have him fly away. Falcons will fly off and today in new territory, different weather, and heavy air the chances had surely been good.

Adam pulls over and jumps out of the truck to check the signal. The wind is picking up and I stay huddled inside. Traffic buffets the truck on the busy road while Adam scans the receiver across the horizon line from the dirt shoulder. Then we're heading in the same direction that I pointed us in the first place. "We'll find him," Adam says, but it doesn't sound reassuring.

"I know. He's got two transmitters on," I answer sharply enough that Adam gives me a quick glare. I imagine he's thinking that I have no right to be angry, that it's my bird and my mistakes that just took off for the beach.

"Here. You take this. My hand is freezing and I can't shift." Adam maneuvers the open antenna of the receiver through the window and awkwardly into the cab, tilting the handle toward me.

I twist the device awkwardly to the front of me and the signal bounces higher on the meter. The gain is set to nine so we're not close to him at all. If we were on top of him the signal would be pounding at three.

We wind down around Malibu Lake and toward Kanan Road, past the Paramount Ranch. I don't know this area well, but I know we're heading toward Thousand Oaks. Adam grew up out here and it seems to me a strange place to practice falconry. There are still open places to fly birds, but all are hemmed in by the movie industry.

In the quick-change charm that's typically California, the land at Paramount turns from grasslands to oak and walnut grove, while streams bend into canyon. This land can transform into anywhere Hollywood's imagination requires. California has been shape-shifted into a thousand places for the sake of celluloid.

The dawn light at the edges of Hollywood is dramatic, a rose glow of possibility, the perfect illumination for endings and beginnings. I can see this even through the sand-pocked windshield of Adam's Tacoma truck. Hollywood was born from this light. Even my untrained gaze sees its magic. Yet, I can't help but think that while Hollywood lulled us into a sweet dream of gloriously lit foreign places, most of California's perfection slipped away beneath the concrete of the film industry. Where exactly out here would a falcon want to go?

Adam pulls over again a few miles up the road. I jump out this time and scan. The wind is whipping my hair into my eyes and I can barely hear the beep of the signal over the traffic. I switch to the transmitter on the falcon's leg, but it's the weaker transmitter and even with the gain all the way up I can't get anything. So I dial the other back in and press my ear to the speaker. We're going the right way, but wherever he's going, he's getting there faster. Someone wolf-whistles and I offer my middle finger without looking to see who's hanging out the window as their car blows by.

"Same direction," I tell Adam as I jump back in the truck, "but we're losing the signal." Adam hits the accelerator and

I wonder, *What's the point of trying to out-drive a falcon?* We catch up with the signal again, though, and I start to think we just might find him hunkered down somewhere. I spend two hours thinking that any moment we are going to catch up to the signal as we readjust our path, weaving through what is now a grid of city streets. "Do you think it's bouncing?" I ask Adam. I've done most of my tracking in the flatlands and it seems odd that we haven't managed to pinpoint him yet.

"I'll get us up on a hill," Adam says. We pass under a stony bridge that could have been built in the thirties and drive twisting and turning up into amazing views and million-dollar homes. We stop in a cul-de-sac that looks over the city and both get out of the truck.

The signal up here is far better than below. I narrow down the location, but don't know the terrain beneath us. "He's down there," I tell Adam, handing him the receiver. "Maybe you can tell where by looking."

"I think I know where he is," Adam says, staring over the top of the receiver into the vague landmarks that must be recognizable to him. So we head back down.

At the bottom of the hill, the beeping suddenly drops out and the sound of the receiver in my lap turns to static. "I lost it," I tell Adam calmly. He pulls over so I can check for a signal outside the dense metal of the truck, but there's still nothing. I call back to Adam from the road, telling him there's nothing to hear and spinning around with the receiver to my ear just to make sure.

Adam climbs out, strides over and then yanks the receiver out of my hand. "Let me see."

"What the fuck, Adam? If there was a signal, I would hear it. I know how to track, okay?"

Adam has this stone expression he wears when he thinks I sound unstable. He looks like he's biting down on his cheeks and his eyes are flat and distant. It's his addressing a hysterical female stare, but it works to quiet perfectly reasonable anger as well. We stand in a deadlocked silence for a few minutes and when he's satisfied I'm not going to say another word, pans the receiver again.

"You probably can't get it from here. I still think I know where he is." Adam hands the receiver back to me and lights a cigarette and I'm not sure if this means he's angry or sure of himself. Either way, we don't pick up the signal again.

I feel sick. It's been an hour of static and hardly a word exchanged between us. I feel like it's me that's lost. When there's a signal there's at least something to follow. The static is like a cloudy moonless night, pitch black. We're making guesses now at where a falcon might go and in the meantime he could be getting farther away and forever out of the receiver's range.

I'm too scared to make a decision which way to turn. My grandmother has only driven me to this church twice and although she explained to me how to walk home, I can't remember if she said the first turn was right or left. I'm only eight and if I make the wrong turn, I may never find my way back home.

I don't like Sunday school and I'm not sure why I have come to the Baptist church where we worry incessantly over the devil's wiles and memorize bits of verse. The only Bible in my house is the one my grandmother gave me for Christmas and no one in my family goes to church. I adore the white leather-bound Bible that zips closed. It's the fanciest book I own, but right now it feels slippery in the sweat of my palm and I wish I could have just read it at home. Maybe if

I offer to read it on Sunday morning, to memorize and recite verses, I won't have to come to this place anymore.

Nothing looks familiar about the street. I finally swallow hard and try turning left, walking purposefully, but with the Bible clutched stiffly to my chest. I make it a block away. Then I pass an unfamiliar pink house with a stretching mulberry tree. I stop to stare it into familiarity, into a road sign, but a lean brown dog rushes from the back, barking and snuffling through the rotting picket fence. An old lady pokes her face out the screen door to examine the ruckus, her mouth twisted with distaste. I panic and run back. I'm already lost forever.

Nobody likes it when I cry, but I can't help it. I have no idea what I should do to get home. While I've paced and panicked, the church service has let out. I wasn't supposed to stay for the service, but I don't see the June-bug green of my grandmother's Impala anywhere. No one is looking for me.

"Sweetheart, what's wrong?" a woman touches my shoulder and hushes me when I startle and cry harder. She manages to ease out my phone number in between my sobs. I hear her on the phone to my grandmother, explaining to her that I'm lost and she needs to come and get me.

I'm too shy to ask the woman's name and she doesn't ask me questions while we wait. She seems to be upset about something, but smiles showing front teeth that overlap when she catches me looking at her. She has a bob of blonde hair, neatly curled under at the edges and a simple blue dress that looks so lovely compared to the red and green plaid of my jumper. I love her shoes too. They are open toed, straps crisscrossing on her perfect little feet. I wish I had shoes like those instead the heavy-soled puke green shoes I'm wearing, the ones that my friend Robin calls my diarrhea shoes. If I were dressed like all the other girls, I might be mistaken for this woman's daughter.

When my grandmother arrives she thanks the woman and laughs, explaining how easy it might have been for me to find my way home. It's only a mile and a half away. The woman smiles back, doesn't show her crooked teeth. When the pretty woman turns away, my grandmother glares at me.

"Adam, maybe we should go back up to that hill."

"You all right?" He asks after taking a long look at me while we sit at a stoplight.

"I just want to find him," I answer.

"And a cup of coffee," he reaches over and squeezes my knee.

"At this point, I'm thinking something a little stronger." I almost push his hand off my knee, but rest mine on top of his instead.

At the top of the hill, outside of the truck, I pan the area with the receiver and in the first few sweeps, I hear nothing but static. Adam is pressed against me so that he can hear the receiver, but doesn't try to take it from me.

"Wait," he says and I freeze, and then swing the receiver back to where I was pointing when he stopped me. I still don't hear anything and then there's a tiny ping. I adjust the frequency, trying to dial it in more cleanly. Sometimes the frequency drifts a bit with the changing weather. Then the ping is back, faint but steady.

"I can't tell what direction. Here," I say, handing the receiver to him. He pauses as if to ask whether I'm sure and I nod. He goes back to the truck and climbs up onto the tailgate to get a slightly less obstructed shot at where the signal is originating. "Is it better?" I ask.

Adam nods, his ear pressed to the receiver. "He's down there." He points and I squint at where he's pointing. "See that fold in the hills? He's right down in there. That's why we couldn't get a signal. Let's go."

He doesn't have to ask me again. I'm already jumping for the truck. I hope wherever the falcon is that he plans on staying, but he could be up and moving any minute.

It's excruciating listening to the static on the way back down to the flats. I don't want to be hopeful, but I can't help myself. Adam seems to know exactly where he's going, but I've already lost my sense of direction. I don't know which way we are supposed to be driving. Then the signal reemerges from the static, faintly at first and slowly getting louder. "We're getting closer," I tell Adam because I'm turning down the gain, fading out the signal as it gets louder so that it's easier to triangulate. I point him to the east and the signal starts to really pound.

I'm focusing on the receiver when Adam says, "Rebecca, what's that?" He's showing me a hundred foot pole with the dark silhouette of a bird perched at its height.

"That looks like a falcon," I say in a hushed voice. Then as the light at the intersection turns green and we pull closer, I amend the thought. "It's my falcon." Adam doesn't say anything, just pulls off the road near the pole so that I can get out and call him down. "What in God's name is he doing here anyway?" I ask, shaking my head at the traffic and the buildings.

"I don't know," Adam says, "but you better get out there and get him down."

I tie some food to my lure and step out of the truck. I position myself in the small field next to the road so that the falcon won't fly into the traffic; then I swing the lure, drop it and pray. I don't need him to chase the lure. I just need him to come down. Then he leans over the edge of the pole, pumps his wings twice and then dives from the height of his perch, a tight, controlled fall that is broken by the stretch and grace of his wingspan a moment before he arrives at my feet.

I immediately hook his anklet to a lanyard on my glove, my hands shaking as I work the French clip onto the open hole of the grommet. I watch him begin to tear bits of quail off the lure, wondering why he looks unfamiliar.

I burst through the garage door. This door faces the gold recliner my grandmother spends most of her day napping in or frowning from, but right now she's wide awake and smiling. "Do you know who this is?" she asks me.

I'm still standing in the doorway, leaning on the open door. There's a woman sitting on the couch across from my grandmother. She's gained some weight and her hair has been cut to her shoulders and permed, but for a moment an image shimmers up from five years before. I see the pixie face framed with long black hair that falls straight down the middle of her back and I answer my grandmother without hesitation, "It's my mommy."

"Come here, sit down," my mom says, patting the sofa next to her and I have to stop myself from running to her. My mom takes out her wallet and shows me photographs of a sister and a brother who were born while she was away. She's married, but everyone wants to meet me. She lives here in town. She says she's lived here all along and she's missed me. I keep nodding and smiling. I can't sort out the new images and information, so I say nothing.

She was lost to me. I've told my friends she's dead because her disappearance was so complete, so silent. Now she's back, but the shimmer I saw when I stood in the doorway is gone. I would rather have this new mommy than no mother at all, but there's a part of me that aches. I think that when you lose someone and they come back, they're different. Everything is different. You don't get back what you lost.

When the falcon has finished his meal on the lure, I step him up on to my glove for a few more bites and walk him back to the truck. I examine him on the way back, his sleek neck and striped tail feathers. I ask myself whether I really know this bird, and whether or not I ever will. For a while I knew his every move and moment. Now there are five hours unaccounted for and I'll never know what happened while we were apart.

I slip on his hood, load him into the truck, and climb in myself with a sigh of relief. Adam leans over and kisses me, then lights a Marlboro.

"Coffee?" he asks. I imagine my African grey parrot at home announcing the dawn and look at the clock on the truck radio. It's noon.

"No, I'm thinking margarita." I say.

"I'm thinking you need to get that bird on the balloon and get a handle on him."

"Margarita first," I say.

CHAPTER NINE

On a Balloon

A falconer named Sterling Jackson has agreed to help me balloon-train my falcon and meets me at a gas station off of Highland Springs Drive in Banning. He leads me up a dirt road into an open field. Though he claims to be sixty, I am told he is closer to seventy. You wouldn't guess. He reminds me of Paul Newman, the piercing eyes, full head of white hair, and face so handsome it defies age. Sterling, though, is missing the bad boy aura. He has a slower smile, a soft voice and doesn't look me directly in the eyes. All the same, when I show him the falcon and we share notes, we are suddenly old friends.

Sterling always trains his falcons with balloons. Falconers have only been using balloons for a decade or so, but it's a straightforward means of teaching a bird to fly high and still think about the falconer. It's target training and the balloon is the target. Sterling is retired and doesn't have a young bird to train yet this year, mine is an early hatch. So he's agreed to help me for the fun of watching a new falcon learn the ropes.

Sterling drives a white Toyota Tacoma like mine, but with an extra cab and a few extra cylinders as well. He needs the bigger engine to tow the trailer behind his truck which encloses the gigantic balloon he reveals inside. Sterling opens the back of the trailer and pulls out a white balloon big enough to get your attention from miles away, leading you to a used car lot or a grand opening. I ask him if balloon-trained falcons ever leave a hunt to follow their training to a grand opening. Sterling laughs. He thinks I'm kidding.

I watch Sterling set up the modified downrigger, a device bolted to a boat and used for pulling up lines when you're deep sea fishing. Instead, our downrigger is mobile, attached to a two-foot-square plastic table, the fishing line ending with a sturdy clip that hooks to the bobbing helium-filled balloon. More strings and a dowel are attached to this setup in a complicated jumble that Sterling promises will work just fine as we hang a rich bit of game bird below the balloon.

Sterling talks slowly and softly, explaining how our progression will go. He sounds as if he is talking to himself and I am lulled by his Southern California drawl. Today we are simply going to let the falcon see the balloon. We'll use a creance, tying him to a line just in case he panics. The balloon is unnatural and to some birds, threatening. If we can just get him to snatch a meal from the string and eat beneath the balloon, then tomorrow we will raise it and see if he will fly up twenty feet to get it. The next day we will go forty, then one hundred, three hundred, and eventually we'll make it to a thousand feet.

The food is attached to the balloon string and when the falcon grabs the food, soaring down, tethered to the balloon by the reward in his feet, we'll reel in the balloon behind him with the downrigger. It's so simple, really. Fly to the balloon and get an easy meal. This is a straightforward way to teach a falcon to fly a thousand feet high, while maintaining some control. At least it seems more practical than just letting the bird loose and hoping for the best.

So with the falcon tied to a line, a short hop to the balloon, I assure Sterling that he will be on his way in a heartbeat, ready for this new phase of training. Despite my assurance, when I slip the hood from the falcon's head, he looks around perplexed. I wait for a minute or so and Sterling raises an eyebrow at me, so I walk him closer to the destination. Nothing. I tell myself to be thankful we tied him to a creance. Whatever thoughts are flitting across his falcon's brain, they probably involve a long-distance flight to nowhere in particular.

When at last the falcon eyes the food, flapping his wings like a test and then leaping to cross the mere fifteen feet to balloon, he doesn't make it. I'm standing on the creance and it yanks him short before his prize. I feel my face flush with heat, apologizing to Sterling instead of my bird and shift my foot off the line. Anakin tries again and this time reaches his meal. An embarrassing start, but a start just the same.

It is a fifty-minute drive to this place west of home and just outside of the desert proper. It's a long drive, but I'm starting to love it. I cross from one world to the next every morning. Out of the dry desert and into the last reaches of the ocean air, the misty cool of the June gloom, its tendrils of fog making it all the way in to Banning. I can see the bank of clouds from miles away, marking the boundary to this foreign place.

My drive starts in the low desert, and when the sun rises I begin to make out the landscape dotted with scrubby plants, creosote, and brittlebush. There are mountains to the north and south, every peak a stretch of new geological design. They cast shadows on the pale sand and on one another, creating a mosaic of earth tones in the rising sun.

From the confines of my truck I feel miniature beneath and between these earthen giants. The approach of the windmills only makes the illusion more grand. The army of turbines rise so far off the gritty desert floor that blinking lights mark their crowns, protecting them from low-flying aircraft. These giants churn constantly in the turbulent air that marks the invisible line that has been drawn between the sandy kingdoms of ocean and desert.

It doesn't end after you traverse through the windmills. Alongside the freeway in Cabazon, a life-size brontosaurus and tyrannosaurus are looming to the north. They have been there for as long as I can remember and I'm sure they are what started my childhood nightmares about the brontosaurus in my father's neglected swimming pool. I've never had any desire to stand beneath them and see how small I am.

From here you drive quickly past the reminiscing monsters and straight into the wall of fog. In the chilly air, I feel myself grow life-sized again, the dangerous journey through the other-worldly complete. I am Alice . . . eat this, drink that, down the rabbit hole you go. And I love it.

Today though, through the fog I could see a balloon hanging in the sky about where Sterling would be. The balloon looks so high that I feel my breath catch and glance at the falcon beside me. Would he make it that far without straying? Sterling doesn't have a bird to fly yet so the balloon could only be set up for my bird. I imagine I will just have to trust Sterling's judgment.

When we are all set up the balloon is at three hundred feet, but Sterling is certain that the little guy will do it. I pull one of the falcon's jesses, slip off his hood, and then pull the other jess. He is half-dressed and there is no turning back now. The falcon watches some horned larks flitting from one patch of stubble to the next. He raises his tail, unloading extra weight from his intestines. Sterling and I both glance down. Birds that are empty have bright green mutes, but the falcon's droppings were mostly white. As we are looking, the falcon takes off from the glove with purpose—in the opposite direction.

I think about the few extra grams the scale had revealed this morning and fidget. Every morning I weigh him, because five grams can be the difference between being interested in food or fascinated by the possibilities of the horizon. So I worry when the falcon keeps heading in the opposite direction. I pull my lure from vest, yell his name and wave my arms. Sterling stands next to me in silence. Then I hear his calm voice, almost too soft to decipher, "He's turning."

I tuck the lure back into my pocket, but keep my hand on it. The peregrine makes a lazy turn a mile away and then heads back toward the balloon with purposeful wing beats. I hold my breath and watch as he comes in, his pitch perfectly matched to the height of the balloon. He binds to the dead starling and slides down the line, landing right next to the balloon rig. The falcon sits tight and easy on his quarry with an attitude which can only be described as smug.

"Thought he was going to fly away?" Sterling asks. He sounds amused.

"Didn't you?" I sit down with the falcon and squint up at him.

"He was just heading out to get some altitude." I nod at Sterling and don't argue. At the moment, flying off and flying up look about the same to me. Someday, the difference might be obvious.

Adam throws back his head and laughs. The lyrics I've fabricated for the Led Zeppelin song are only mildly amusing, but his laughter is contagious and I cough as the tequila I am sipping burns down the wrong pipe. It isn't what I said that makes me laugh in return. It's the stretch of Adam's neck laid bare and vulnerable, the joy of having captivated him. I love it when he laughs and he seems to do it so rarely.

I have fed up my falcon and am taking a few days off from training because so far he's doing fantastic. So this weekend, I don't have to worry over the peregrine. I can just enjoy my boyfriend.

Adam and I are watching a short video that he's put together of his red-tailed hawk hunting in the American River Canal. The sand verbena is so thick on the desert floor, a purple carpet I can still almost smell. The hawk twists and turns, a jack rabbit the size of a small dog evading her moves with impossible timing. This dance is always over so quickly that we never catch the rhythm in the field; it's all blur and drama. On digital video, slowed to match a beat we can fathom, the hawk and hare slow into reality. It's breathtaking, even though the hare gets away, and the next two as well.

The final flight is a rodeo, the struggle matching the swelling music. The closing footage has Adam wrestling with the hare, smoothing the way for the tired hawk. I know that I held the camera for this shot and I feel a blush of ownership. In the shot Adam wipes the sweat from his forehead and then turns to the camera to wave victory. It's a juvenile gesture, but the editing is so clean, the landscape so stunning in its lunar sheen that Adam's awkward glee is forgivable. He really is an amazing video editor.

"You should try to get a gig with the Outdoor Channel," I tell him. "They would be insane not to hire you." I mean it as encouragement and a compliment, but Adam frowns.

"I couldn't give up falconry for a job," he snaps.

"I understand," I say because I wouldn't give up falconry either, but really I don't get it because I work a full-time job and write books on the side. Why does falconry exclude working for living?

"Besides, I couldn't leave here," he finishes and then shrugs.

"Really?" I ask, looking around at the tiny dusty space he rents and wondering why he wouldn't want to leave. He knows what I'm thinking and frowns at me. I'm killing the laughter.

"Hide out here as long as you want. I know where to find you," I say and wink.

"I'm not hiding," he says, grabbing a pack of cigarettes. I watch him step outside, closing the door behind him. I suppose he means to protect me from the cold air outside, but I think he also means to shut me out and I turn away from the closed door. I find myself wondering what you gain from the solitude of an eternal hunting season when you can never return from the wilderness. I want to ask him, but I never was any good at reasoning with men.

"We need to use a cup on the balloon," Sterling says and I shake my head at him, disagreeing. We've got the falcon flying eighteen hundred feet high and need to transition him off of the balloon.

"Are we watching the same bird? Even if you cover the food, he will never look down if there's something to fight with up there." I have my hands on my hips, I've made up my mind, but Sterling is certain he's right.

"Tom says you should use a cup."

"I know," I answer. I've talked to Tom as well. I talk to him at least once a week and every other week we disagree about something. I keep wondering when he's going to stop taking my calls.

This is the hardest part of balloon training. We need to get my bird to look down, stoop his prey below him and work me back into the picture. I've got his pitch. He is as high as I want him to go. Now we need to phase out the balloon. He needs to fly up and then look down to see what prey I have flushed, what is flying below him.

Normally, what the guys do is fashion a cup above the food on the balloon. Right before the falcon gets there, they drop the cup with a remote release, covering the prize. Then they have to hope the falcon will look down as they flash a pigeon to get his attention—that the pigeon presents a better meal below.

This all sounds reasonable to me, except that I know this bird. He won't forget there is food under the cup and he will battle with the cup to wrest away the food beneath. He will do this until he finds a way to foil our system and get his reward. Then I will have trained a bird that never looks down and never gives up.

"We'll just send it up dry, Sterling. He'll go up and there won't be anything to mess with when he gets there."

"He'll see there's nothing there from the ground."

"He'll go anyway," I say. Sterling doesn't answer and I think to myself that we aren't bickering because I'm wrong. We are arguing because I'm not doing as I'm told.

"I know I haven't done this before, but it won't hurt to try."

"Fine," Sterling says. "It's your bird anyway." He has already told me several times that my falcon is likely to fly away if I choose to do this. He also already knows that I don't believe him. I believe that some birds do. I just don't feel that mine will.

I nod and walk away, sighing. I know he could be right. Sterling is already wearing his "I told you so" expression as he puts up the balloon.

The falcon looks up and even at eighteen hundred feet away, surely sees there is nothing on the string, but leaves anyway. Habit is a powerful thing. He mounts the sky fast and isn't happy when he gets there. He is too busy pondering how to get a meal from the balloon to look down. Even with no food up there, I can't get his attention.

I want to glare at Sterling, to wipe the "I told you so" off his face with a sharp look, but I am too busy trying to figure out what to do. Then the falcon's wing beat changes and I know he has his own idea.

I watch the peregrine make an outrun, a flight out in an effort to come back higher and know exactly what he is thinking.

"Oh, man," I sigh. Sterling asks me what I'm worried about and I shake my head. It is a clever idea on the falcon's part, but it will never work. The peregrine comes in above the balloon and I know he is going to land, but there is no way he would be able to balance, right? He flutters then, like a songbird perching on a millet feeder and disappears at the apex of the balloon. I burst out laughing. "He landed on the balloon, Sterling."

"No he didn't." Sterling gives me a look, half disbelief and half further irritation.

"If you don't believe me, pull the string. He'll slide off when you tip the balloon."

"It isn't possible," Sterling insists, but I shrug and gesture toward the downrigger and the taut string that stretches from it. Neck craned, Sterling walks to it and gives the string a yank. My falcon slides down the side of the balloon, grabbing with his feet and stretching his wings, and then regains the sky with little grace.

It takes some effort to get him down even after this. He is certain the only way to get a meal is from the mouth of the balloon. A half an hour later, I finally have him on the ground eating a meal from the lure. He has made this difficult, but I am completely enamored with his creative thinking and determination. I made the right training decision, but Sterling still doesn't seem convinced. I wonder what he's going to say when I tell him I think the next step is to get rid of the balloon altogether. Tom Austin is going to disown me.

Adam and I stand in the cool morning beach air in a field in Camarillo. Despite our long chase and my poor attitude toward my falconry friends, Adam seems to have the utmost confidence in me. Everyone else has made it very clear that I am making a bad decision.

I know I am rolling the dice after our last tense tracking session. Adam could have voiced his concerns and changed my mind. Instead, he picks a field where we will have an easier time tracking a bird and crosses his fingers with a conspiratorial smile. This is falconry. This is life.

I release the falcon and he makes a tremendous outrun, disappearing on the horizon. Adam keeps him in his binoculars, but with my bare eyes I can't make him out.

My heart drops when Adam tells me that the falcon is stooping something. He is hunting away from us, without us, and is probably not coming back. I refuse not to hold out hope though. I will my peregrine to find his way back to my truck for a meal. Adam has a pigeon tucked under his arm and we were ready to serve him a meal, just like a real hunt, if he will only come back.

I pull out the telemetry receiver and dial in the signal after we have been patiently watching fifteen minutes for his flickering wings and listening for the ring of his bell. My heart is slowly pushing toward my stomach. I don't want to track him, but already promise to be kind to Adam, not to argue and make this an ordeal if we must. I still have a signal though, I just can't pinpoint where it is. It isn't close.

I hand the receiver to Adam. He pans it and can't figure it out either. The signal seems to come from everywhere. Maybe I should have just listened to everyone and done what I was told. Adam shakes his head at me, noting the signal spikes once in a while, that it just doesn't make sense and then his eyes go wide.

Adam points the receiver directly above him into the sky and signal pounds. Our eyes follow the direction of the antennae and find the flashing silhouette of a peregrine one thousand feet directly above us. We stand in mystified silence and then I start shrieking.

"Serve him. Serve him. Throw the pigeon!"

Adam responds instantly and the falcon tucks his wings, rocketing from the sky. He falls long enough to count seconds and as he gets close I can hear the wind whistling through his feathers and bell. He is falling so fast he sounds like jet craft and isn't slowing down. Then suddenly there is a concussion in the air above, an explosion of feathers and my small falcon is on the ground next to me.

I grab Adam and kiss him. Then I release him to jump up and down, yelling our triumph back into the blue. Adam laughs and shakes his head. "I don't think I've ever been kissed by a falconer. Not even when everything went right."

The falcon settles in to eat, close enough to touch even after owning a sky so large that it was difficult to spot him, let alone coerce him. I didn't see him on the horizon, couldn't find him to call him back. So instead, he has found me. We're ready to start hunting together.

Chapter Ten

To Catch a Goshawk

"You're doing what, now?" my mom asks, perplexed, and I'm not sure exactly how to explain it. I've never watched someone pull a goshawk out of a nest. "Why doesn't he just buy one?" my mom asks sensibly.

"If I could trap a peregrine on the beach, I would," I explain. "It's illegal now. My only choice is to buy one from a breeder. A goshawk, though, you're allowed to get one from the wild." People buy goshawks as well, but I'm certain that nature is the better breeder. So I don't explain this. "I'm not saying I would rappel down a cliff to pull an eyass falcon out of the nest. If Adam wants to climb up a pine and pull an eyass though, I want to see it."

"That'll be interesting," she says, and the way she says it makes "interesting" sound sexy. We like men that are braver and stronger than us. Then she pauses, switching gears. "I have to ask you something," she says, and her voice catches.

"What?" I'm already cringing. I knew she had an agenda when she called. She just happened to ask what was going on with me first. So I told her I was taking a few days off to go up north with Adam to get a goshawk. I was hoping we wouldn't come back to this. I have a feeling I'm not going to like the question.

"I've been thinking a lot lately and I have to ask. You've got to tell me the truth, okay? I just have this feeling and I need to know." She pauses, gathering the strength to ask this question that I may not be able to answer. "Did Clyde molest you?" She spits it out in sharp syllables and it's done.

I'm silent for a moment. My options are all loaded. I'm not convinced my mom won't get back together with my stepfather. I don't know how any answer will affect my mom. So I say the thing that pops into my head, a growing mushroom after a long-gone rainstorm. "No." Then I say it again, "No, of course not."

"I just got this feeling . . ." my mom says, but she sounds relieved. I want to make her feel even better.

"It was weird when I was a teenager . . . I mean, you know. He wasn't my dad; he was my stepdad. And I was just such a flirt. I was afraid you would think . . . I don't know, Mom. It was just weird."

"Oh, thank God." My mom sighs and I imagine her wiping away the tears. "I was so sure. I'm just . . . I'm glad I asked. I'm sorry I asked, okay?"

"It's fine, Mom. I'm glad you asked." I hope that my smile is sincere enough to be felt across the phone lines. "Look, I have to be somewhere in a few. I'll call you tomorrow, okay?" My mom has no objections to that, and when I hang up the phone, I pour myself a glass of wine and sit down on the couch.

My stepfather hands me a glass of white zinfandel. We just came back from Nordstrom and I can barely keep myself from rifling through the bag of clothes. I think about them as I sip the wine and how gorgeous I'm going to look in the cropped flower print pants and the pale blue satin shirt. Everything is Easter colors. Everything is floral. I'll look like the other girls in high school. No one will point me out as a freshman.

"The thing about love, Becky, is that you never want to be the one who loves the most."

"What do you mean?" The wine is making me feel light on my toes, but that still seems a strange thing to say, especially since we're talking about his relationship with my mother.

"The person who loves the least is the person who's in control. Even if you love more, don't ever let your lover know." His eyes are wide and lips pursed, like he's told me the secret to life. I wonder what this bearded man, eyes shielded with wire-framed glasses, and more than ten years married, could possibly know about love affairs. I humor him.

"So you don't love Mom as much as she loves you?" I look over the rim of my wine glass like a woman who's mastered sipping and flirting. And I'm pretty sure that I have.

"Well, we have sort of a . . . mutual arrangement." He smiles when I widen my eyes. "Well for example, at the company Christmas party, I made out with another woman."

"And Mom's okay with that?"

"Of course. She was in her office making out with another man." He waves his hand like it's no big deal and I try not to scrunch my face for fear of giving away that I don't understand the adult world. "Finish that up so I can rinse it out." He points to my wine glass with a conspiratorial smile. I know he means to dry it and put it away before my mom gets home with the kids.

I think about how much I hate white zinfandel now and pour myself another glass of merlot. It was the right thing to say to say to my mother. I'm sure of it.

It's a seven-hour drive to Strom Greer's house, but Adam and
I never run out of falconry stories to swap. Strom is a falconer
who lives in a simple trailer in the woods and we are immediately met with affection from his family. Strom has four children with exotic names and wonderful temperaments. He's a
single father who somehow manages a true falconer's life. His
family doesn't have a lot of things, but they have everything
they need and a great deal of Strom's time. Strom isn't there
when we arrive, and Adam and I are offered beers by children far too young to drink, but well-taught in good falconer
manners. Adam roughs up Wolf's hair and tells me about the
ten-year-old boy cleaning and cooking a pheasant for him on
his last visit. I'm smitten and Wolf knows it. He brings me
another beer.

Strom and I have never been introduced, but he is unmistakable in the falconry crowd. I recognize his slim gait and
his Fabio hair when he jumps out of the truck that arrives,
welcoming us both. Unfortunately, he doesn't have good news.
He was out searching for nests with his apprentice. He talked
to a biologist that they bumped into in the forest and it wasn't
a good year for goshawks. A heavy and late spring snow had
likely caused a high percentage of nest failure this year. That
meant less young and less chance that Adam might find a near
fledgling chick. All the same, Strom knew a nest that was successful every year. He didn't check it, but he would take us to
it in the morning. It was likely that Adam would still go home
with an eyass.

My hope for Adam turns to vertigo the next morning when I
see the seventy-foot pine he is about to climb. I listen to Strom
explaining the climbing system, how to hook up the ropes and

wear spikes and I realize that Adam has never done this before. I'm terrified for him. All the same, I realize that if I wanted a goshawk more than anything in the world, I would convince myself to climb that tree. So I brush his cheek with the back of my hand and politely ask him not to fall.

Adam is scared too. I know him well and can see him grapple with his fear along with his equipment. He keeps his sense of humor, though, calling down to me to ask if I could bring him up a drink of water. Half way up the tree there is no reason to be amused. An active nest would involve two parents trying to knock the falconer out of the pine.

This is the thing I don't understand about flying a goshawk. They are a bird from the genus Accipiter, a crazy faction of birds. In fact, the falconers that fly them are really no higher ranked in sanity. We even have a special name for these falconers, "austringers," and the accipiters they fly are profoundly excellent hunters. However, their drive and instinct to hunt replaces some of their intellect. They catch first, think second.

I like to say that they "see dead people" because with no notice at all they become terrified of the most average thing: a plastic grocery bag floating in a field, a falconer's new red baseball cap. She will fly away from you for hours, always a step ahead until she has forgotten that something terrified her in the first place.

Accipiters also have a reputation for aggression. Average aggression involves getting yourself hurt when you're trying to help your hawk with a meal. An accipiter that has not been properly raised will likely leave her kill on the ground to bind to your face. It's an unpleasant way to lose an eye or a piece of your lip.

This same propensity for aggression has damaged many a falconer robbing a goshawk nest. The moment a chick has disappeared from the nest the parents will forget. In fact, they'll have a much easier time finding food for and raising the remaining one or two eyasses. If you don't have to though, you really don't want to be up in their nest. You need to wear a heavy jacket, a construction helmet and your best game face. I've heard many a story of a goshawk making a grown man cry for mercy. As big as a red-tailed hawk, but agile, they are a formidable adversary.

Yet Adam is halfway up to the nest and no parents have appeared to protect it. We all know what this means, but if you're halfway up the tree there's no reason not to finish the journey. We know, but wait until Adam glances into the nest and his curses ring through the pines. The eggs are bad, probably chilled in the late snow. The hen had abandoned them. There are only a handful of days left in our legal eyass season. Adam and Strom are going to have to come up with new options quickly.

We arrive back to Strom's exhausted and unhappy, but make a few phone calls to other falconers and after a few drinks, rally our spirits. In the morning Jim Garamond, another austringer, calls us, but can't meet us. He sends a map to work with his wife instead. We catch up with her late in the morning at the city office where she is employed. She could have been put off by our desperation and dirty clothes, but instead offers us the map, and her home where she has left the door open. There are clean sheets as well as a shower and food if we want to stay the night. She isn't a falconer, but she is undeniably an excellent falconer's wife.

Adam, Strom, and I follow the map, and walking through the forest, play a tape of goshawk calls on a boom box. If the territorial beast has a nest anywhere near, they are sure to reply, complaining about the intrusion. Yet the forest is silent.

We are fresh out of ideas and I am supposed to be at work the next day, a twelve-hour drive from where we are sitting. We have come so far and tried so hard to find Adam a goshawk. So I don't mention my pending schedule and focus instead on how we might make this work out.

"Let's do a Hail Mary," Strom says and we listen while he explains what he is thinking. It was a poor goshawk year and likely the only people who know where the nests had actually been successful are biologists. If we want this information we have to go to a ranger station. The problem is that for the most part, California Fish and Game still hates falconers. However, Strom makes a few phone calls from an old fashioned booth and we are soon on our way to pick up a map of a successful nesting site.

We get our map at the ranger station and run into a group of kids in their late teens and early twenties who have spent all day surveying nests. They are dusty, their clothes grungy, but they seem friendly. They give us more directions to what they say is a much better nest. The one we have a map for is one hundred feet up a rotten stag. They tell us to follow their new directions and then the pink markers they have tied to the tree branches. Suddenly our adventure has surely been saved, or so we think.

We follow their notes and find a pink marker and then another and another. We find thirty markers and no nest. I fight motion sickness, cramped in the back of the extended cab of Adam's truck and stay silent, forgotten by the men. Adam broadcasts goshawk calls and hears nothing. The young biologists are probably laughing at us over their pints of beer right now. Our options for Northern California are exhausted.

I'm a day late to work when Adam and I leave the next morning. Still, there are other possibilities and other places where I might see my first wild goshawk. Next weekend is the last few days of the season we are allowed to pull eyass hawks legally. I figure we will find someplace else to go then.

Back at work I tell my story of tree-climbing boyfriends and treacherous biologists. I'm still hopeful for Adam. There are other falconers that know of nests and might be willing to share their location. Then the phone rings at my desk and it's Adam. "I'm on my way to a nest right now," he says.

"Where?" I ask, disappointed.

"I can't tell you," he answers softly. I understand that goshawk nests are secrets kept between the best of friends, but I'm uncertain why in the world you can't tell your girlfriend.

"Come on, Adam. Who am I going to tell?" I meant to be understanding, but it blurts from my throat with a bitter taste.

"It's in a California mountain range, I can't tell you more than that."

"So it's close. You could go this weekend?" I ask, more of a suggestion than a question. I really do want to see a goshawk. I've still never seen a wild nest and I feel like I've put in my time in apprentice and girlfriend hours.

"Stan and I are going right now. Stacey can't come either." He says this so I know that it's boys only. Stan's wife Stacey is a falconer too, so I should understand, but I don't.

"I understand," I say and hang up the phone.

CHAPTER ELEVEN

Fighting for Control

"So Adam got a goshawk?" my mom asks.

"He wanted a female, but there were only two males in the nest. He thinks they're a little old, but it was his last chance, so he took one."

"But he didn't take you with him."

"I had to work," I say and wait for my mom to protest. Instead she notes how lucky Adam is to have a falconer for a girlfriend. Then she asks me how my falcon is doing.

"Fine," I say. However, it's far more frustrating than fine. I'm working on teaching him to hunt doves, but it's a challenge and a new one at that. Sometimes he tries and sometimes he ignores me and mostly we're getting nowhere.

My mom and I talk about the weather, we talk about her quilts and the wine we're drinking and then we run out of things to say. Mom lets me go with only a tiny hesitation, wanting to believe that we aren't talking because we've run out of conversation. I know better. There is much to say. I just can't say it. So I sit on the couch and think about the falcon instead.

I managed to get him off the balloon. I still have to drive an hour to find a field to fly because I haven't yet found a suitable dove field in the desert. However, in Banning there are some open fields filled with doves and possibilities. The falcon takes a nice pitch and holds well, waiting for doves to break beneath him, but they are harder to catch than I imagined. Doves know to stay out of the air if there is a falcon above and will not come up from the stubble of a field unless your boot brushes so close to them that they give in to their panic. If the falcon clips them in the air, they spin, falling to the ground and into safe hiding again where the falcon cannot find them. These doves aren't injured, just holding tight in the hopes of remaining undiscovered. I know this because I have re-flushed them, walking through the field once the falcon is back on the glove and the skies are once again safe for flying prey. I'm worried my falcon will decide that I am an unworthy hunting partner and stop trying.

"You just need help flushing," Sterling says. "I'll bring Sasha and we'll help you." I agree, but doubt that Sterling and his dog will do much good. I'm losing the falcon's attention. Yesterday he gave up on me and landed on a pole. I don't want my falcon to learn to do this, to sit on poles like a lazy red-tailed hawk and wait for a convenient meal, but at least he's not flying away.

At the field the wind has kicked up and Sterling questions whether I want to do this. It's blowing at fifteen miles per hour, tough to fly in. I tell him the falcon has to learn the wind, because the air won't always be still. I don't want to be one of those falconers who don't fly their birds, choosing not to hunt every time the situation isn't absolutely perfect. In the wild, falcons have to hunt in the turbulent air.

The peregrine rises off my glove and is blown downwind. He wobbles and struggles in the difficult air, uncertain how to manage. He fights his way back upwind to us and then lands on a pole, perplexed. Sterling shakes his head. "That's not good."

"He's just thinking," I snap. "Give him a chance to figure this out." Sterling shrugs and we wait to see what the peregrine will decide to do. The falcon sits for a while, but then decides that he will give it another try. He wobbles again in the stiff breeze, is swept to the east and then gets his bearings. As I watch, he learns to work the unsteady air. He glides downwind and then turns his face into the rush, pumping his wings and using the resistance to give him lift. It doesn't take long before he makes it to a thousand feet and is waiting on above us.

"Let's do it," I yell to Sterling and he releases his dog as we start running the field. I had seen doves put into the clumps of black-eyed Susans, the yellow blooms springing up in the sun-baked winter wheat. So I head for the nearest patch of flowers, but find nothing. Sometimes the doves just dematerialize when the falcon is in the air. I never see their escape. Looking up in the sky, I find the falcon but he is upwind from me, which is why the dove in front of me breaks from the ground at my feet and whirrs into the air. The musical clap of dove wings is unmistakable and I call out to the falcon, but he doesn't have the slightest chance. The mourning dove whips downwind too fast for the falcon to close the gap between them.

I'm yelling my frustration into the sky at the birds when I hear Sterling adding to the din. "Two more just came out behind you!" I spin around to look, running as the falcon stoops, close enough to tail a dove this time. The peregrine matches every twist and turn the narrowed-winged dove can manage. Pushed by the gusts, the chase is happening in double-time. Sterling fumbles his binoculars from his vest as they fade out of sight. "He's on her tail, still chasing, stooping, chasing, oh! She burned him."

"Damn," I sigh, but pull out the lure. It was a great chase that deserved a meal just the same. So I call down the falcon and end the hunt.

"Tom says you should put him back on the balloon," Sterling notes as I'm feeding the panting falcon.

"What?" I ask, wondering why in the world Sterling would say that. The little falcon is trying so hard. Surely, we'll catch a dove any day if I keep having hunts like this one. Why would we go back so many steps in training when I actually have him hunting?

"He's landing on poles. That's a real problem," Sterling says and I wonder if he noticed that I didn't ask him for advice, only for help flushing. Then I wonder why everyone feels they need to share notes about what I'm doing in the field. I don't care if he lands on poles as long as he gets in the air at some point. I want to remind Sterling yet again that this is my bird. I scraped to do it, but I paid Tom the full thousand dollars for this falcon, yet everyone wants to make decisions for me.

"I'm going to find a place in the desert to hunt doves," I say, thinking that I am tired of everyone watching and manipulating me. "It's too far to keep driving out here."

My grandmother calls me out of my room, yelling down the hall, "Your daddy is here. Come out and talk to him." I perch in one of the recliners, attentive and ready for small talk as if we are entertaining a guest. My dad asks me about school, if I have done my homework, and then he asks how my weekend with my mother was. When I tell him that my stepfather said he would take me flying, my father's eyes look through me and his jaw tightens. "Absolutely not," he says and I can't stop the disappointment from spilling down my face. I hadn't meant to make him angry.

"You went to ground school," I sniff. "You like planes."

"It's dangerous. You tell your mother I said you are not allowed to go." My dad looks away from me, then gets up and leaves, slamming the door behind him.

I climb into my stepfather's Cessna and smile at him. I shouldn't be flying. Clyde knows this as well, but points out that what my father doesn't know won't hurt him. When I had realized it would be just us in the two-seater plane, not my brother or my sister, I had to go. I want Clyde to like me. I want him to want me to be his daughter. I want one of my parents to claim me, so I decide that I love planes too.

He has rented a Cessna 150 to do a night flight out of the tiny Riverside airport. If we time it right, we will make it to Anaheim and get to see the fireworks at Disneyland. He says he will let me steer and show me how to do a "touch and go."

The plane is loud and bumpy, but this is new and wonderful and none of my friends have ever flown in a small plane. None of my friends have seen fireworks from above instead of below. I'm imagining the stories I will tell, how impressed everyone will be. Then I realize I won't be able to tell anyone. If my grandparents find out they will tell my father. And when Clyde smiles over at me, I wonder if he hopes that I will tell them anyway.

When we're in the air I stare out the passenger door window, into the Lite-Brite design of countless city streets and houses below. The noise of the engine makes it too loud to ask anything but necessary questions, so I just imagine how I would describe the twinkle of landscape if I could tell someone. I'm leaning against the door when it pops open.

My view is suddenly unobstructed, endless and I want to lean out farther to see more. Then I'm pulled back into my seat. I turn to look at Clyde who isn't panicked. He's smiling in a way that doesn't seem very friendly and points at my seatbelt, yelling to pull the door shut. I snap on my belt and then wrench the door closed. Clyde reaches over me to check that it's secure.

"Did it scare you?" he asks and I think about his smile, nodding that it did. That seems to be the right answer. I wasn't scared, though. I was thinking about how free I could have been if I would have just leaned a little further and seen more of the lights.

Once I start looking, it doesn't take that long to find places to fly near my apartment out in the desert. I discover a couple of alfalfa fields that have doves flying in at dawn in flocks of thirty and forty birds. They are open areas in the middle of the agriculture and will probably work well. It's a half an hour to drive out to Thermal and Mecca, but that isn't far and at least there are options. However, it's the field on 52nd Street in La Quinta that makes my heart race.

It's only a fifteen-minute drive from my apartment. There is a pond on one end, so some of the doves come in for a drink of water. Then there is another open hundred acres, perfect for flying and there are thousands of doves here. This, I think, will be where everything comes together at last. The falcon and I will learn how to hunt together in this field.

"It's perfect, Adam. I know I'm going to catch doves there," I tell him breathlessly when he calls that night.

"That's great!" he says and pauses. "I have some good news too." I wait for him to tell me, although I don't like the way he says "good news." He already sounds like he's trying to convince me of something. "Stan got me a job working at Sexstatic."

"Porn," I say. I want to yell that we agreed he wouldn't do that, but I realize that we never agreed to anything.

"It's great money. I have to do this for us. We can't live together if I don't have a job," he says, like it's the most reasonable thing in the world.

I start to say that it's okay. I'll make it work somehow, find a way. Then I realize that I shouldn't, that I can't. I want to be supportive, to be open-minded, but I feel sick when I think about hearing the stories from work and having to have "colleagues" over for dinner. "You do what you think is right for you. I won't date someone that works in porn. I've been really clear on this."

"Don't be like that," he says. "It's not like I'm going to be talent. I'm just editing."

"Talent," I say.

"The people are really nice, Rebecca. They're just normal like you and me. Stacey is fine with it." He's getting angry now, rationalizing. He's thinking about what a prude I am and how unreasonable I'm being.

"Stan's wife doesn't know what they're getting into," I reply.

"And you do. You know better than everyone else," he says and I flinch at the sarcasm.

"You know I do," I say quietly.

"Stripping is not the same," he says. I swallow hard and shake off the tears that are starting. I've already lost.

"I've spent a lot of time with strippers and I know what they're like. A lot of them end up in porn. I also met plenty of porn stars when they came in for—special engagements."

"You just don't trust me," Adam yells.

"Why the fuck do you think this is about *you*?" I scream, and Adam slams down the phone.

I curl up on the kitchen floor and sob. He doesn't call back, and I know I'm not going to change his mind. We've been talking about moving in together and I thought it was what I wanted more than anything. Now I won't be moving to Los Angeles where there is cool air for the falcon and a handsome falconer in my bed. I crawl past the parrot cages, into the bathroom, and throw up in the toilet.

I'm twenty-one years old working in a strip club to make ends meet. Pia pops a half a tab of X in her mouth. She is splitting it with Veronica. It's against the rules to do drugs when you're on the floor, or even drink alcohol, but I'm probably the only one here that isn't drunk or stoned. I'm having a bad night, too. It doesn't look like I'm going to get my quota in dances or the overpriced sodas the guys are supposed to buy us. If I don't make my quota, I'll leave owing the club. If I'm lucky the bouncer and the bartender will mark them in for me, but they'll expect a hefty tip the next time I have a good night. The DJ has already written me off for decent tips. He hasn't given me a good light show on stage in weeks. An awesome light show can really make a difference in the number of lap dances you get in a night.

"Bitch, who said you could play my song?" Brittany screams at me as she strides into the dressing room. I take another drag off my Camel and don't look up.

"I didn't know you owned any songs, Britt." I should just say I'm sorry, that I won't do it again. She's pissed or high and is probably having just as bad of a night as me. Yesterday though, Angelica took a swing at me because I did three dances for her best customer. I'm tired of putting up with the shit from these women.

"I'll just kick your ass right now, skinny white girl," Brittany seethes. Pia looks up wide-eyed, but doesn't say anything, just sprays on more perfume, adding to the crazy mixed-up scent of this tiny room.

"What's going on in here?" the manager bursts in. He's got a keen ear for screaming women. We all shrug and ignore him. "Berlyn, get your ass out there. You've been in here for at least twenty minutes and last I checked your card, you weren't having much of a night." He's talking to me, but I don't respond immediately to my stage name. None of us have real names and I often forget mine.

I stub out my cigarette. "I'm going, just let me freshen up."

The manager leaves and I'm a couple minutes behind him. Brittany pushes me when I walk by and hisses, "If I were you, I'd have a bouncer walk me out to my car tonight."

The next morning I wake up with the alarm and silence it with a groan. I'm certain that if I move an inch to the left or right that whatever evil has settled in my stomach is going to find its way out again. So I lie very still and tell myself that the falcon can take a morning off.

When at 6 AM the bells of my restless falcon begin, the guilt gets the better of me. My falcon has no idea that my life is tearing at my guts. He only knows that he desperately wants to fly. I listen to the bells and think that I want him to fly too. I don't know if we'll sort out how to work together, but right now he is the only honest, predictable relationship in my life.

CHAPTER TWELVE

Giving Up

Every morning is a maybe and maybe must be enough for now. The falcon is so close to taking game. I am so close to being his real partner, his provider, the one that flushes the dove that ends up in his feet. Each morning I wake up believing this is it, the start.

I am certain that the field in La Quinta with the small pond, lined to the east with tamarisk trees, to the south with ten-foot-high thorny hedges, and smattered with scrappy orange trees, is going to seal my future. The doves arrive at daybreak every morning to sift through the soil with their delicate beaks. They must feed on the fruit or maybe depend on the safety of tamarisk and hedge, but something makes the field attractive. I'm certain all I have to do is convince the falcon to wait on above and our success is assured.

I get to the field in time to watch the quality of light change. When the air brightens and shadows can be delineated from darkness, it's clear enough to hunt. Pulling out the receiver, I check for a signal from his leg mount and then a signal from the tail mount. Both are strong and I leave the receiver set to the stronger transmitter on his tail. I strike the braces, pull off his hood, and beg silently for success.

The falcon doesn't disappoint, taking to the sky with an earnest desire to climb. I don't need him too high, four hundred feet should do. I'm watching him, my breath catching, heart pounding, because it's looking so viable, so possible. I can imagine the flush of doves, the fall of the falcon, the exhilaration of success. Three hundred feet, one more turn in the sky, and I'll make my way to where the doves are beneath him.

One last check of my pockets and I find a lure and some quail in the right, the binoculars in my left. I'm about to stride forward when the falcon flies into the sun that is just peeking over the horizon. Trying to look after him, the glow blinds me for moment. Turning away, I try to blink off the red haze. When I look up again, I can't find him in the sky.

He was almost in position, but I don't see him now. I can't hear his bell. It's too hard not to panic. This was supposed to work out. Fumbling with the receiver, I get a signal in the direction I last saw him and it isn't moving. I'm confused, but then imagine the best possible scenario. He's caught a dove on the ground. Better if I would have been there, but at this point any little success would be a huge one.

As I'm tracking, it seems that my hunch is correct. The signal stays steady, there's no fade and spike of a circling falcon. He's somewhere close and not moving. I only worry for a second when it seems to be originating from the thorn-laced hedge. The picture I attach to the beeps becomes clearer. Somewhere within the safety of the hedge, my falcon is scattering dove feathers, probing for the dark meat below.

I don't find dove feathers. What I find are the perfectly painted feathers of juvenile peregrine, a handful of body feathers that never rip loose without trauma. As I absently stroke one of the soft round feathers in the palm of my hand, a winged shadow passes ponderous and silent in front of me. As I look up to the broad wings of a red-tailed hawk, my chest constricts. Where is my falcon?

The receiver is certain the falcon is in front of me, but it takes a few minutes for my terror to fade and to think this through clearly. I try to rip into the place where the signal seems to be the strongest. The bushes are too thick and the inch-long thorns rip at my skin, leaving bloody bite marks. There's no falcon in this dense and nasty hedge. Somehow he's left the tail-mounted transmitter behind.

It's okay. There's a transmitter on his leg. I flip the receiver from the "six" frequency to the "one" frequency. Nothing. I turn up the gain all the way. Spinning, I look for a signal in any direction, but the only thing to be heard is static. I've lost a half an hour looking. God only knows how far the falcon has flown. I'm sobbing as I sprint for the truck. He's not supposed to keep flying off.

He was headed into the sun last I saw. Maybe he kept going east. Maybe he's too far away for a signal. If I keep driving I might pick it up. I hold on to this hope for another half an hour, before I admit the truth. I'm searching blind. I don't where my falcon is and may not find him.

I've lost birds without a signal at bird shows. We've always found them and I tell myself I'll find my falcon too. He's been tracked a dozen times now. Sometimes he stops on those hundred foot poles in Indio. Sure, there are hundreds of poles, but at least that's somewhere to look. At a show we would all go out en masse, even call everyone who's off for the day. The only person I can call now, though, is Sterling and I dial his number into my cell.

"I've lost my falcon and I don't have a signal."

"That's bad. Is it dialed into the receiver right?"

"Yeah. He left the tail mount behind. I'm not getting anything from his leg. I'm blind here. I need help." There's a long pause on the other end and I wonder if Sterling is thinking of who else I might call to help.

"Well, I've got to go grocery shopping. What's the frequency on his leg mount? I'll climb up on my roof later and see if I can get it."

"You . . . Sterling, you're forty miles west of here."

"Well, he might head back this way." Sterling sounds chipper, like he's convinced himself that climbing on his roof is a helpful solution.

"Never mind, Sterling. I'm sure he went east." I snap my phone closed and squeeze my eyes shut against the ache at my temples. So it's a solo effort, just start scanning poles for dark silhouettes with pointed wings.

Driving, I can't help but wonder what happens if I don't find him. I want to believe the falcon is going to be fine without me. It's not like he hasn't caught food on his own. He's proven to be an excellent pigeon assassin, but he's still a baby bird. He doesn't know the variety of ways the world can kill him yet. I wouldn't be the first falconer to find nothing more than feathers, feet, and transmitter beneath a satiated red-tailed hawk. I don't know if the falcon understands that he must be on the lookout for other predators if he has something desirable. I've got to find him.

A man in a grey Chrysler pulls up along the curb, behind my grandfather's blue Datsun pickup. I can't really pay attention to what he's doing. I have the loose end of a ball of twine tied around my dove Aerial's right leg, the balled end under my foot. I'm trying to coax her to fly to my hand from a slender branch in the mulberry tree that dominates our front yard. I don't know how to train birds, but repetition makes sense to me. Maybe if she learns that she only owns a twine's length of sky and the comfort of my palm, she'll choose my hand forever.

"What are you doing with that bird?" The mans calls to me from his car. He looks old to me, a faint touch of grey at his temples, but he's smiling and really wants to know.

"It's a ring-neck dove. I'm training her."

"To do what?"

I shrug and pluck her from the tree branch, feeling self-conscious. "Nothing."

"Come here. Let me see her." He's beckoning with a friendly hand and seems sincerely interested. Despite the grey, he's handsome, with straight teeth and dark eyes. Maybe he's only thirty or so, I'm not so sure. I hold Aerial squirming between my hands, but close to my chest as I approach. "How old are you?"

"Thirteen." I blush, realizing that he's looking at my breasts and not the dove. I should really be wearing a bra, the shape of my adolescence is obvious under my tank top, but I haven't been able to convince my grandmother to buy me one.

"What's your name?"

"Becky."

"Becky what? It must be Irish. Look all those adorable freckles." He has such a nice smile and no one has ever called my freckles adorable.

"O'Connor."

"I've never seen that kind of dove before. Have you ever seen one of these before?" He gestures to his lap.

I lean in a little to look. His pants are undone, his penis lying flaccidly on top of his right leg. I shrug, "Yeah." Then I turn to leave. "I've got to put my bird away."

"Wait, Becky. Can I call you?"

I don't know how to answer that so I shrug again and wave goodbye, running up the driveway. I stay in my room for the rest *of the afternoon and try to put the image and its implications out of my head.*

My grandfather seems confused when he yells for me to come to the phone. I pick it up in the den and when a man groans, "I want to fuck your tight little—" I hang up.

Back in my room, I know who called. A last name and a street address are enough to get my grandparent's listed phone number. I'm shaking. I should have told the man, "No. You can't call me." It's my fault.

"That wasn't a boy was it? Why did a man just call you?" My grandfather stands in my doorway.

"I don't know," I answer with a steady voice, but my grandfather looks at me like I'm lying. Still I lie again, saying "nothing" when my grandfather asks what he said. If he keeps pressing for answers, I'll tell. I'm a terrible liar and I know I'm about to be in so much trouble.

"Fine." My grandfather shakes his head, done with questions, and leaves me alone. I hear him grumbling to my grandmother in the living room that I wouldn't tell him anything.

"Well, she must have done something," my grandmother growls over CNN. "Men don't just call little girls." Then my grandparents stop talking. I sit on my twin bed, legs crossed tight, and will the phone not to ring again.

I've been looking for three hours, drawing a grid of Indio in my head, trying not to miss a single street. Making the paces, my eyes have blurred and the static blaring from the maxed-out receiver is making my sinuses ache. Calling in to the zoo, I say I don't know when and if I'll be in today and no one gives me a hard time. I'm going to have to give up this pointless pursuit eventually, but I'm not sure when to make that decision. He could be out by the Salton Sea, maybe he headed toward the windmills or the Santa Rosa Mountains. There is no way to know, only to hope that the lure of pigeons in semi-suburbia is the most desirable of these possibilities.

Many first-year falcons are lost in a fly-off. First-year falcons die so many different ways. Dan O'Neil lost a good hybrid last year. That bird was tenacious and talented and had the promise of many great seasons in its snappy wing beat. There was nothing Dan could do when the pigeon crossed traffic, the falcon oblivious to anything other than the thrill of the chase. There was no possibility to best the Peterbilt. The pigeon pitched up and bounced off the windshield. The falcon was crushed against the grill, a kidnapped corpse, nothing more than a trail of juvenile feathers left in the wake.

Vince Andrews nearly made it through the season last year with his bird flying a mile high and knocking prize after prize from the sky. She was a Peales peregrine with a nasty temperament, but a hell of an aggressive hunter. There was only a week left of duck season, just a few more days until the safety of the off season. They were flying at a pond that had power poles along side of it. Vince meant to flush the ducks away from the lines. Most came off in the right direction, but one green-winged teal shot beneath the wires. The tiny duck must have looked like too much of a prize to do anything more than pull the trigger. The falcon stooped without seeing the lines between the duck and the fall. She sheered off her right wing on a wire, tumbling to the ground, her life wasted.

Last year Sterling even lost Pepper, a bird with a decade's worth of seasons under her wings. She was training on the balloon, but checked off on what he thought was a pigeon or dove, typical behavior for a bored or perhaps slightly fat falcon. When she didn't come back to the balloon, Sterling went looking. He found her on a mallard, the duck half-eaten and the falcon dead. She seemed untouched except for her broken neck. Sterling didn't see a raptor fly off as approached, but heard the whine of a coyote in the distance.

Maybe it's not bad falconry. Maybe sometimes it's just bad luck. Falcons aren't infallible and neither is telemetry. There were fresh batteries in mine. I checked them before I let him loose. They should be working, yet I can't help but feel this is my fault.

There's something in the distance on top of a pole. It looks like a falcon. I've been squinting for so long that I don't trust my blurry eyesight and don't get excited. It's probably a dark prairie falcon, or perhaps I'm totally off the mark and it's a pigeon. The sun is nearly central in the sky and I know my chances of finding the falcon are poor. So I don't believe it even as I pull underneath the bird, even as I raise my binoculars. I don't believe it until the binoculars focus on the transmitter hanging from his leg. My receiver is still blaring static, but there's no doubt that I am looking at my falcon.

I cheer loud enough to drown out the buzz that's been the morning's anthem. No one finds a falcon without telemetry, especially a first-year bird. He could have been anywhere, but he's here.

Getting out of the truck, I yell to the falcon, but he only gives me a cursory over the shoulder glance. Then I realize I'm in trouble. He's caught something and the bulge of the meal he consumed looks like a softball under his chin. There is nothing in my arsenal or any other falconer's bag of tricks enticing to a falcon that has gorged. I know I'll never get him down, but try anyway.

I try first with a dry lure, feeling silly even bothering. Swinging the lure, I yell, but don't even get a glance from him. He's got a foot up, preening the feathers on his chest. I tie a whole quail to the lure and swing it again, dropping it beneath him. He looks at me this time, but not with interest. I'm bothering him. So he bumps, flying to the next pole. I try again. He bumps again. It's pointless.

A moment ago I couldn't believe my luck, now I can't believe I'm going to have to sit under this falcon until tomorrow when he's hungry again. I climb into my truck, cursing this ridiculous sport. Without a signal I can't leave him. There's no way I would ever get lucky enough to find him twice.

Pounding on my steering wheel, I growl my frustration at the windshield. Then I lower my face into my hands and push back the tears again. Nobody said flying a falcon would be easy. Nobody ever claimed that any sort of living would be easy and I chose the challenge. Dropping my hands away, I take a deep breath, brace for the long wait and glance up at the falcon, but the pole is empty. The falcon is gone.

I bury my face in my hands in earnest this time. Why did I find him only to lose him again? I'll circle around the block, but I know what I'll discover. He's gone. There will be no finding him now. Driving around all day hoping for a glance of a bird that doesn't want to be with me is pointless. He has no use, no need for anything on the ground. I sob into my palms, pitying myself for hinging my happiness on something as unpredictable as a falcon, for chasing things that belong to the sky.

I tell myself, No more tripping over the things in my path while my eyes are to the clouds. Enough. It's over. I take a quick turn around the block, confirming what I all ready know, the falcon is truly gone. There is no point looking anymore and I head in to work. The falcon and I will both be fine on our own.

CHAPTER THIRTEEN

A Fighting Chance

At my desk I keep telling myself that this is for the best. My bird show boss was right when he wouldn't let me fly the falcons at the Toledo show. I would only have lost them and surely they would have died.

We lost a Barbary falcon in Florida before leaving for Toledo and he was dead before the next day. I wasn't the one flying him, but was just as desperate to find him. Barbarys are tiny falcons with flashing eyes and a hunger for as much sky as you'll let them master. We let the falcon master a little too much and the bird became overzealous, leaving us all behind.

We tracked him immediately, without waiting to see if he might turn back. The flash of his wings and focused path out of our sight told us he wasn't heading back for anything. Our only chance was to stay beneath him and lure him down. It took all day for the falcon to come down, but it was of his own decision. We tracked him all over Winter Haven and Lake Wales, through the sand ridge and eventually into the swamp.

It was too dark to see into the cypress by the time we had a close-range signal. We were wearing waders, but that didn't stop the mosquitoes from coating our throats and cheekbones. The falcon couldn't see us and there wasn't a dry place to call him down to anyway. We had no choice but to come back in the morning.

At first light we discovered that the signal had moved. It was still in the swamp, but further to the north. We figured he had just been bumped in the night until we found the transmitter. It was in the dark water at the base of a cypress, still attached to a falcon leg, owl pellets floating nearby in the murk. We only looked at the nest above for moment. Great-horned owls are supreme predators and there was no need to deconstruct our loss.

Still, this falcon is different. This falcon is tough. I've seen him scrap with a wild prairie falcon twice his size. He's caught pigeons and must know how to avoid bigger predators, how to keep from being eaten. If he does get hungry though, will he know to stay away from people? Falconers accept that our birds are part of the cycle, but sometimes it's other people that damage and destroy our birds.

When I was an apprentice I heard a story told around a campfire. A falconer lost what he swore was one of the best falcons he had ever hunted. He spent two days tracking, never quite pinpointing where the bird had landed. When at last he had a solid signal, it seemed to be coming from inside a ramshackle house. It was the sort of house we're particularly familiar with in Southern California, with its sharp chemical smell and ramshackle isolation. It was likely a meth lab. Not the best place from which to save a falcon.

The falconer knocked and a man with a pocked face and twitchy hands answered. The man said there was no falcon and slammed the door. Checking the telemetry, there was no doubt the bird was inside.

The falconer pleaded, swore he wouldn't cause trouble, promised that all he wanted was his bird. He explained, his face pressed to the door, that the falcon had given him twelve phenomenal seasons, despite a wing injury in her first. The falconer pleaded that he had no children, this bird was the closest thing, but the door didn't open.

The falconer started pounding on it. He demanded his bird, threatened to call the police. In retrospect it was the stupidest thing he could have done. The people inside took him at his word and inside there must have been panic. The falconer got no response and hadn't really planned to call the cops, until he checked the signal. It had changed. It was coming from beneath the street, from the sewer pipes.

He did call the police and as he suspected, it was a meth lab. He had prayed the tweakers had only flushed the transmitter down the toilet, but they were flushing pieces of the falcon. How do you explain to a beloved falconry bird not to trust all humans? How do you explain it to anyone?

Sometimes my stepdad stays up late with me, like tonight. It's one o'clock in the morning, my half-sisters, half-brother and mother all in bed. We were watching The Serpent and the Rainbow, *a movie I'd been wanting to see, but my grandparents don't let me watch things on cable. It's not that they worry about my viewing, just that they dominate the living room. There's some other movie on now, some late-night weekend nonsense. Clyde is tickling me and I try to get him to stop and not make a lot of noise at the same time without much success. He just keeps jabbing his fingers into my sides while I squirm and giggle.*

I hate being tickled, hate that it makes me laugh when I want to scream. I'm not strong enough to make him stop and he always tickles me until my eyes water and I feel like I'm crying. My mom doesn't like that he does this to me, but she doesn't make him stop. I want to be a part of his family, so I don't make a fuss about it either.

He finally stops the tickle fight and I catch my breath sighing. Lying down next to me in the sofa bed, he strokes my legs and I let him. I'm wearing my nightgown, ready for bed. The nighty is long and flannel, hardly sexy, but at sixteen every move I make seems sexy. He pushes up the skirt to my thigh.

His fingers brush up my thighs and I can't help the sensation that spreads warm through my belly. I want to be touched, to be loved. So I don't stop him when his fingers slide under the elastic of my panties, between my legs and probe inside me. My mind spins and I don't know what I'm feeling, until my mom calls out from down the hall. "Clyde, are you coming to bed?" Then what I feel is fear.

He leaves me without glancing back, like a man caught, but prepared to leave the evidence behind, talk his way out of it. I hear them arguing on the other side of the house and wonder if my mom is going to throw me out. This is my fault. I can't walk into a room without looking to see who I can seduce with a glance and a bounce in my step. I brought it on myself.

I ask the oldest of my sisters in the morning if my mom is angry with me and if she's still fighting with Clyde. She is only eleven and looks at me perplexed, then later tells Mom what I said. My mom approaches me carefully, like a bird that might startle to flight and asks why I think she's mad. I don't know what to say.

I know what to say now, even though I didn't then, even though I didn't know what to say when my mom got up the nerve to ask if Clyde had ever touched me. My face is in my hands again and I'm getting no work done. I don't know why I bothered to come in.

"Are you okay?" Jennifer looks into my office, her dark hair pulled back from her face, her huge brown eyes concerned. She's wearing the zoo standard, khaki polo and shorts, a treat bag on her belt that she's forgotten to take off after the show. There's a slight bow to her stance, an animal trainer sensing a problem that merits running.

"I lost Anakin. I have to get him back. Can you help me?" I say it before I realize I want to find him, but I say it and I mean it.

"Yes," she answers immediately. Her stance relaxes as she waits for orders. Jen got the job supervising the show at the zoo, a job I was certain I should have had. It chafed so much that I took a position in administration, managing the publications and grants, utilizing my degree in writing. Truth was, the hours and pay were better than Jen's, but we had both been trying to make amends ever since.

I explain to Jen that there's no signal and he has a full crop. Since he gorged he might not go that far. Wherever he is at dusk is where he'll settle in for the night. If we can find him somehow, I should be able to get him back in the morning. We swap cell phone numbers and start looking.

I don't cling to hope, but feel better for making some sort of effort. Maybe the falcon won't be found. Maybe he won't make it, but I'm searching, I'm trying to find him. At least Anakin has someone looking out for him.

There's less than an hour of light left when my cell phone rings. I answer it, wondering if Jen is giving up on me.

"Don't get too excited, but I think I'm looking at your bird." She knows it's a raptor, is pretty sure it's a falcon, but the light is fading and she can't see if it has equipment on. They're only two blocks away.

I don't get excited, but I hold my breath until I get there. When I look up I let it out with a "whoop." It's him. It's Anakin. Twice a needle in a hay stack.

I hug Jen. Looking at Anakin's crop, I explain that I'm unlikely to get him down until he's a little hungrier, but that's okay, he'll be hungrier in the morning. My cell phone rings again and I glare it.

"What do you want, Sterling?"

"I'm on my way out there. Where are you?"

"You're . . . what? Where have you been all day? Never mind. Do you at least have a pigeon with you? I'm going to need one." I tell Sterling where I am at even though I know he's not going to make it in time. When he arrives it's too dark to do anything. The falcon is asleep on a pole right outside the Indio Country Club. Nothing will get him down until morning.

I take the pigeon Sterling brought, then I send Sterling and Jen home with my thanks, although for Sterling they are hardly sincere.

In my truck I sit under the sleeping falcon for a while, wondering why the Barbary falcon we left out in Florida was eaten by an owl. Was it his bell? Did he try to move in the dark?

I could stay beneath him all night, but I can't protect him from here. And if he bumps, I won't be able to find him again in the dark. The only thing I can really do is go home and come back before dawn, hoping for the best. In the bird training world, we call this putting the bird to bed. So I say goodnight and head for home.

This certainly isn't the first time I've left a bird out. I know what I'm in for. The night will be long. I'll check the bedside clock every half hour if I'm not already staring at it. When I sleep, it will be for twenty minutes at a time and I'll dream I've slept past dawn and the bird has already flown off. Still, the alarm will work. I'll get up in time and be awake before he is.

At home in my apartment, staring at the empty screen perch, I pour myself a glass of Charles Shaw merlot. I take a few sips and pick up the phone. Dialing my mom, I take a deep breath.

"Hi, Mom."

"What's wrong?"

"I lost Anakin today." I tell her the story of the morning's fly-off and the double miracle, but I don't tell her that for a while I gave up. I don't tell her that he could still be eaten by an owl. There's something else that needs to be said. "Mom, do you remember when you asked me about Clyde and if—well . . . ?"

"Yeah," Mom answers in a tight voice. She knows what I'm going to say. She knew all along or she wouldn't have asked the first time.

"I lied. I'm sorry. Maybe if I would have just told the truth a long time ago it would have been over sooner. You would have found out about the other family sooner."

"He would have said you were a liar. He might have done anything to keep from losing us. I would have believed you, but it still would have been hard, especially on you."

"Still, I wish I had been braver."

"You sound plenty brave to me." There's a long silence while we both discover there's nothing else to say. "You better try to get some sleep."

I have two glasses of wine and sleep amazingly well, considering the possibilities. I don't wake until the alarm beeps its annoying staccato at 4 AM. I arrive a half hour before the sun is even threatening to illuminate sleeping silhouettes. Sitting in my truck with the binoculars continuously at my eyes, it's an excruciating wait. For a while I think he's just the shape of my imagination until at last there is no question. The falcon shifts, straightens a few feathers on his back. I'm in business.

He doesn't look at me immediately, but when he does I know he's going to come down. It just takes some time and coaxing. He doesn't eat any of the food I have to offer him, but drinks when I squirt water into his mouth with a spray bottle. He feels heavy on my glove, the meal he's consumed a palpable feast. He lets me put the hood on without any fuss and I sigh when he's tied to his perch in the truck.

On close inspection, he somehow managed to break his BP transmitter. The tailmount is missing from his deck. He didn't lose a tail feather, then, but I'm going to have to find the transmitter and put the mount back on. It's going be a few days before his weight is back to where I would trust him to fly anyway.

I wonder what happened to him out there. Did he chase a dove and crash into the tremendous brambles? He's missing a few feathers on his chest. Peregrines don't crash into bushes. It isn't their style. Was there a battle? Or did he just get the urge to head toward the sun? I wonder what he caught as well. Was it a pigeon or something bigger and fiercer? And was he smart enough to eat it somewhere safe? These things, I suppose, are not for me to know—are better for me not to know. My job is simply to find him, to try to help him get home safe, to teach him to trust me and then to set him free again.

PART II

CHAPTER ONE

Unlikely Saviors

"Where do you think it is?" Tom Austin asks me this and motions at the hedge in front of us. I flip on my receiver to double-check.

"It's on our side of these bushes, three-quarters of the way up." I gesture to a place that's about eight feet high. "I think it's right here. I just can't see it."

Tom flips on his own receiver to decide for himself. He's driven two hours to meet me in the desert where I've lost Anakin's transmitter. I had looked all afternoon but couldn't pinpoint its location. I didn't want to give up on a two-hundred-dollar transmitter, but I never thought Tom would drive all the way here to help me. I had only called to tell Tom about losing and finding the falcon, about getting Anakin back. When I told him I hadn't been able to locate the transmitter he asked what the frequency was, what exit to take off the freeway, and then said he would see me in a couple of hours. "Don't you want directions?" I had asked.

"Nope, I'll follow your signal," he had answered. I was worried that he would show up and pluck the transmitter from the bushes from somewhere in plain sight, but he seems to be having the same problem I am. I'm relieved that I am not an idiot and that I really did need help with this.

"It's right where you say it is," Tom says. "I'll go get my hedge clippers."

"You brought them?" I ask this because I thought he dismissed the suggestion when I made it. Living in an apartment I had no need for hedge clippers, so I didn't own a pair of my own.

"I turned back to get them." He pauses to study my face. "I figured if you said we were going to need clippers to get to the transmitter, you meant it."

I suck in my lower lip as he walks away because I don't want to smile, but I'm about to grin ear to ear.

Tom returns with the clippers and asks me to point to the agreed-upon coordinates. Then he starts clipping. "You weren't kidding, this stuff is nasty," he says. He's got as many scratches on his arms as I do now, blood oozing at their edges.

"What do you think he was doing in there?" I ask, thinking that Tom will surely have an answer.

"Why do they do anything?" he questions instead.

I keep waving the receiver while Tom hacks at the stand of twisting thorns. After twenty minutes or so, it seems that we should have the transmitter, but can't see it anywhere. It's somewhere above his head, but we should be far enough in to spot it. And then I do. "It's right there, Tom."

He follows the line of my finger and squints into the brambles for a while and then he sees it too. It's hanging from a branch, antennae pointing to the ground at about ten feet high. Tom reaches for it, but even his eight foot reach isn't going to be enough.

"Maybe I could grab it with the clippers," he says and tries, but it's too awkward.

"How about a stick with a piece of gum stuck to it?" I offer. Tom grins.

"Got any gum?"

"No, I don't chew gum." We both stand with our hands on our hips, gazing up into the bush, sweat licking dust tracks down our faces and necks from the late afternoon sun.

I try getting into the brambles, but the branches aren't strong enough to support my weight. They snap and give and I can't get any closer than Tom did. "I think you're going to have to lift me up there," I say.

Tom's expression is thoughtful. "You sure?" he says and sounds a little shy.

"If you could just support my weight a little . . . " Now I sound shy too. We're going to have to work together physically to get it. He's driven two hours. I've been trying all day and we're looking right at it. So we get over our embarrassment.

Tom puts his hands around my waist and I climb up into the stand of shrubbery. We've cut to the trunk of the strange biting bushes and with some support, I am able to use the inner branches as steps. Stretching as long as I can make my body, I trust Tom to balance me and hold my weight. My fingertips brush the transmitter and I stretch a little further, then it's in my hands. "I've got it!"

The awkwardness between us is gone. Tom sets me on his shoulders, an easier way down, and walks me out of the tangle, lowering me onto the ground. We high-five, gather our tools, and walk back to our trucks. It was just a transmitter, but it feels like a tremendous triumph in the face of a difficult two days. "Thanks," I say.

"You're welcome," he says. "Now what are you going to do about the peregrine?"

"Try not to lose him again," I say and Tom gives me a fatherly frown. I look into the sky, but there are no falcons and no answers in it. "I don't know." Yet I think that Tom might have the answer, that he might help and I'll listen.

I've been getting strange calls for a week now. I'm seventeen, so getting calls from males that sound like men is not unusual. These aren't calls from boys in my high school, though. They are all men and the calls are lewd. They keep talking about the things they want to do to me. It isn't like I haven't heard this all before, but I've had enough. So I'm ready to tell this strange voice on the phone where he can put that ridiculous piece of flesh between his legs.

"You sound young," he says and I'm formulating a snappy come back as he continues. "You should know that there's some . . . unsavory writing about you. I was calling to tell you so you could do something about it."

"What do you mean?" I ask because all the insults I've gathered have evaporated.

"It's in the men's restroom at Sears. The one on Arlington," he says. "Do you have a brother or someone that can take care of it for you?"

"I'll find someone," I say, although I can't think of anyone.

"Be careful," he says and hangs up.

I feel worse than after the obscene phone calls. I didn't feel violated before, but now I do. My grandfather is the only person I can think of to help and I'm certain that's not a good idea. All the same, my choices are limited. I don't want anyone reading whatever is written on those walls, but someone has to erase the words. So I go into the living room and tell him.

When my grandfather returns he is practically shaking. "Do you know who wrote those things about you?" He asks. I shake my head. I honestly have no idea.

"What did it say?" I ask even though I don't really want to know.

"Never mind," he says. "I took care of it." His eyes are sad, but he's not angry with me. I think he wishes I would have asked him to take care of me sooner.

"Have you looked at this pond?" Tom asks. I shake my head no. "Some good ducks there. Let's go look."

We climb into our trucks and pull up to the pond on the other side of the field. We roll down our windows to talk and Tom glasses the water with his binoculars. "Cinnamon teal, mallard, and gadwall," he says.

"It's too close to the road, right?" I ask, thinking that I'm not sure I want to hunt ducks. My peregrine is so little and they look big.

"No, this is totally doable," Tom explains and describes how I would flush the pond. "Doves are hard. Most peregrines don't manage them until their third season. Your little guy's got heart. He could take ducks. They're big, but they're an easier target. Give it a shot."

I'm nodding my head, looking out over the pond with my own binos. Why not hunt ducks? Isn't that what I've always imagined? A peregrine stooping from a thousand feet to knock waterfowl from the sky.

"You and Adam getting back together?" Tom asks and when I look up he is still staring at the water and the bobbing ducks.

"No," I say, remembering the final goodbye, but keeping the story to myself.

"How could you do this to us?" Adam asks. We're standing on the doorstep and we've been talking for a half an hour. We aren't getting anywhere. I drove all the way out to try and explain what part of this is killing me, but it hasn't gotten me anywhere. I wish he looked sad, but I think he looks angry and that can only mean that he isn't hearing what I have to say. He's just blaming me and wondering how I could do this.

"I don't know," I answer even though I really do know. I say this to stop myself from saying that everything will be fine and I'll get over it. I want to bend and give up the fight, let it go. So many other people make concessions for people they love. Why can't I? Then I imagine the people Adam will be working with calling on the phone or showing up for a dinner party and I feel sick.

I want to take him back. I want to take everything I've said back, but instead I scrub at the tears beneath my eyes and turn away. He slams the door.

I don't know if I'm forgiving everyone and moving forward with my life or blaming Adam for everything and condemning myself to solitude. It doesn't make a difference though, because either way, it's over.

"That's too bad," Tom says and this time he does look at me and his expression is melancholy. "Two falconers, I mean. You both really seemed to get along." What he's doing is asking me why, although he's not sure he wants to know and he is certain he doesn't want to get involved.

"He took a job editing porn," I say waiting for his reaction. I don't want to speak poorly of Adam, but it's important to me now that Tom understands that I didn't make the decision on a whim. The rest of the gossiping falconers think I have. "I'm not opposed to the product. It's just that . . ." I trail off because I hope I don't have to explain.

"You have to follow your heart," Tom says, an approving but intense expression on his face. Then he looks back at the water. "You should hunt ducks. Find some more ponds." Tom doesn't have any children of his own. He helped raise his wife Jenna's son from another marriage, but there were no other kids. Tom says his birds are his children. I study him now and think there is a part of him that is reluctantly paternal.

"Okay," I say smiling, because what I really hear is, *Get back on that horse.*

Duck season is just about to start so there's no reason not to try. I should get a duck stamp, my first duck stamp, I think and wonder if we'll fare any better with waterfowl. I start to think we couldn't do worse, but know better than to tempt the fates. Hunting ducks in the desert. It seemed like a contradiction. It seemed—right.

"Let me know how it goes," Tom says, nodding. Then he drives away.

CHAPTER TWO

Mi Casa Es Su Casa

"You have to see this quilt," my mom says, describing her new-est cathedral windows quilt. It does sound amazing and my mom sounds completely sober, so I grab a Diet Coke from my refrigerator instead of a glass of wine. "I booked two more lectures today too."

"You're on a serious roll," I say, and I wish I was in the same position with the peregrine. Still, I haven't given up yet.

"No duck yet, huh?" She sounds disappointed and I think she wants the peregrine to succeed as much as I do.

"Not yet, but we had a discussion about it," I tell her, laugh-ing. My mom wants to know what I mean. I don't "talk" to animals. I'm not anthropomorphic, but Anakin's personality is starting to really shine through.

Yesterday morning at the pond in La Quinta, the peregrine decided that I should flush the ducks, push them off the water before he gained any sort of height.

I spent too long training this falcon to fly a mile high to let him mug his prey from a pitiful pitch. So I stood at the edge of the water, arms crossed and waiting while he glided ten feet above the water, occasionally trying to pluck a web-footed feast from the water. The ducks submerged and reappeared in ran-dom places. I wasn't helping, the ducks weren't budging and Anakin was frustrated. He landed on the top of my truck.

At this point I lost my head too, berating my falcon like a lover or a child or any other disappointing English-speaking primate. I screamed at him to get back in the air, gesticulating my desires with waving arms and skyward jazz hands.

The falcon didn't give me the response I wanted. Instead, he bowed his head, raised his tail and began to scream back in the shrill tongue of peregrine, both our voices escalating. We could have been a couple arguing over who was doing the better job of shirking their responsibilities, if only we had been speaking the same language.

Then I realized I was quarreling with a peregrine and began to laugh. The peregrine hushed and studied me, his head tipping in interest. Wiping away my tears and clutching at my aching abdomen, I wondered what the peregrine version of a great big belly laugh looked like. I waited for him to get on the wing again and called him down for a quick meal. We could try again another day when we were in agreement.

"So you got into a fight with your falcon?" My mom asks.

"Not exactly," I say, but I'm glad there were no witnesses.

"I'm really sorry about Adam," she says. I sigh instead of answering and she continues. "You made the right decision. We should do a better job looking out for ourselves." She pauses and then adds, "For each other too."

"You should come visit," I say.

"Or you could come here," she replies although she is aware she's never been to visit me anywhere and that she should. "Someday you'll have your own house and I'll come visit then." I agree because I really want a house of my own, but wonder why that should make a difference.

At the pond in La Quinta on yet another morning, I am cautiously hopeful. At the very least the world looks promising in the dawn light on wild desert. I can hear larks singing in the field, and I spot a handful of ducks on the pond. I'm not very good at duck identification yet, but it is easy to spot the green heads of two drake mallards. The brown ducks at their sides are likely the less flashy females. There are no ducks half their size, so I know there is no teal. I'm pretty certain, though, that the ducks with the black tails are gadwalls. Tom told me gadwalls are a good duck for a baby falcon.

The falcon is so high once he finally gets going on the wing. I cannot watch him and try to flush ducks at the same time. And the ducks aren't too willing to come off the pond. It's a little pond. I could throw a rock across it if I didn't throw like a girl, but the ducks are more afraid of the falcon than me. It takes a lot of commotion, rock throwing and splashing to get them to move.

This is the down side of hunting alone, but I'm glad there is no one else out in the field with me. I don't think I want anyone to witness my ineptitude yet. Still, I keep stopping to check the sky, worrying over whether he's still with me. I can't keep my eye on him and finally give in to the realization that I should really call him down to reward him for staying with me as long as he has. I make the decision too late though. I have already completely lost him to the sky.

Back in the truck, receiver on, I start tracking. This isn't what I wanted to do with my morning, but I've tracked him before and will find him again. I stay on top of the signal, but he zigzags through the agriculture, making the chase difficult. Following the pounding signal down the road, I am sure I am going to see him any minute.

The only straight road that leads toward the signal of my missing falcon is wet. A farm worker had turned on sprinklers a few minutes before and they douse the road as well as the newly planted crop. I consider the possibilities and think I can pass unscathed. It is a half a mile of road that is quickly getting wetter, but I gun my engine despite my familiarity with the glue that is created when you mix water with this sandy soil.

Halfway down the road my back tires go out from under me. There is no going back and the paved street is 250 feet in front of me. I make my way a foot at a time, moving forward, sliding sideways, backing up a little, moving forward again. My tires spin and the sprinklers force me to turn on my windshield wipers just to see.

I'm patiently trying to make progress even though the signal is fading and I know I'm not progressing nearly quickly enough. Then my truck tires spin and don't stop until my engine stalls.

I rest my head on the steering wheel and think to myself that I should forget about it and stay stuck. Enough of this, but the signal is still fading, so I grit my teeth and get out of the truck. I roll it as far as I can, inches, but just enough to move me a little further. Then I do it again and again. It takes a half an hour and a couple more rolls in neutral, but eventually I am on the paved road.

I hadn't looked back the whole time I was fighting the muck, but from the road I steal a glance. There is 250 feet of deep slithering ruts in the road and the whole world seems covered in mud. I could find something in my childhood to compare this to, some moment of crisis that has colored my life but I don't want to. I take a deep breath and pull out onto the pavement determined to find my falcon.

When I get on top of the signal again, I don't like it. It doesn't make sense, fading in and out. I triangulate the source of the beeps on my receiver. There are pigeons amid the houses, but the signal isn't from the ground, so he hasn't caught one, but I can't figure out where he is.

I drive down a dirt alley toward a handful of leaning mobile homes, past three signs that tell me in Spanish and English that I am trespassing. He is somewhere in between here and the road. I stand in the alley next to a wall that separates the road from some ramshackle buildings, brandishing the receiver and cursing. Then there is a sound like wings to my right.

I turn and find myself facing a panel of chicken wire, my falcon inside hanging on the wire with desperation on his face. If I didn't know better I would say they are pleading eyes, begging me to save him from whatever situation he has gotten himself into.

"Hang on," I say, knowing he can't understand and laughing nervously because he is hanging on. I sprint down the alley to my find my way into his prison and to seek out the people who own this cage. There are pigeons in it, a perfect meal for any falcon and I think through my pathetic command of Spanish trying to figure out how I am going to explain this.

The man I find at the front of the property is in his sixties, a caballero, well-dressed and wearing a fine cowboy hat. His beard and mustache are neatly trimmed.

"Mi halcon esta alli" I say, pointing to his yard.

"Tu halcon?" he asks.

"Cazar patos con mi halcon, porque . . . " I struggle for the word for pigeon. "El quiere tus pigeones." Close enough.

"He's with my pigeons?" the caballero responds kindly in English. "Go ahead." He gestures in the direction of his backyard through a wrought iron gate. "Go get him."

I find the pigeon loft in the back, past several holdings that must have held cattle or horses.

The loft isn't closed but the pigeons are too alarmed and my falcon is too greedy to find their way out. He hasn't caught anything. He just sits on the ground, panting with terror and exhaustion. I feel the same. Some men are as serious about their pigeons as I am about my falcon. In some lofts my falcon would have already been killed by the pigeon racer simply for his predatory audacity. I can't say I would blame the pigeon guy either. A winning racer might pick up twenty thousand dollars in a big race. Still, I am shaking with relief.

It takes ten minutes before the falcon will even consider eating. He just wants to ride home to the familiar on my glove and I just want to take him. We are both shaking just a little.

When I introduce my peregrine to the man whose home he has invaded, the caballero tells me in Spanish that this handsome falcon can come calling anytime. "Mi casa es su casa," he says.

I shake my head "no" and smile as best I can. One of these days my bird might not return from someone else's house. I wonder why I do this to myself, but know I won't quit until the falcon makes me. In some ways I feel this is all I have left, a tenuous bond with a foreign soul. We'll figure it out. And maybe we'll always find our way home.

Chapter Three

Grounded

I dream of a small pond planted in the center of the sprawling desert agriculture with a single duck bobbing at its center. I dream of this because Tom Austin keeps telling me not to give up, that the ducks will arrive soon. We've been trying for three weeks now without any luck. Tom keeps telling me I will find a single dark coot floating in a pond and my troubles will be over. No falcon could resist a single coot laboring on its short wings, its tiny head bobbing as it crosses an open field. If I can find a setup like this I can explain to the falcon through example what we are trying to do.

The problem is that I don't know this desert, this odd slice of the Sonoran where farmers have harnessed the Colorado River and funneled it into agriculture. They grow artichokes, alfalfa, carrots, onions, cilantro, and romaine. There are acres and acres of table grapes, crusted white salt flats filling the spaces in between. Nearly every field has a small open reservoir at one of its corners, a reservoir with reeds, duckweed, and flowing water. We are only fifteen miles from the Salton Sea where waterfowl stop over by the millions during the migration. Surely there must be ducks enticed into these ponds from time to time.

I peer over the berms of ponds every morning, hopeful and careful not to be seen just in case there are some waterfowl in the water. I keep hoping, but my hopes are taking a beating. The desert is an adversary I don't understand and I'm starting to hate it. This is not unlike the six months I spent in Australia hunting with a goshawk. I hated the Australia bush much the same way. Murrindindi showed me how to listen and connect. I wish I could find a Torrez Martinez Indian elder to do the same in this desert that should be home. I wish someone could help ground me.

➤

Murrundindi plays the didgeridoo as campfire shadows dance on the canopy of gums above us. His face is striped and spotted with red and white, the face of an Aborigine, one of the last of the Wurundjeri. The deep voice of the instrument, a hollowed eucalyptus branch, weaves through the sacred smoke in a sensual song. There is no melody, but you feel the words with your entire body. It is the voice of a world graced with wings and safe pouches for the young. Even in the darkness you know that you are protected within the song of a didgeridoo.

Murrundindi is performing a grounding ceremony for me because he knows I have having trouble connecting with the land and hunting with my hawk. Hunting with a hawk in Australia is nothing like hunting at home. My heavy-winged American hawk and I had conversations in the field, calling back and forth while we worked the land. The chaparral spoke to me. I could feel when the wind was going to change. I could guess within a day of the next rainstorm. And I often knew when there was a rabbit hidden at my feet.

None of this is obvious in Australia. I feel like I am blind-folded and stumbling through the lower hemisphere and I regret coming here to work at the bird show and rehab strange Australian raptors. I can't seem to get grounded.

My Australian goshawk and I have a trepid relationship, not unlike any two foreigners speaking different languages. I coax her with food and repetition, calling and whistling my intentions. Yet she mostly ignores my voice, cueing only on my movements through the eucalyptus. Sometimes she flies to my glove for a bite of meat. Often she changes her mind halfway. Sometimes she chases the rabbits running in front of us. Usually, she watches instead. I want her to depend on me to flush her quarry, to believe that I will let her chase it, and to trust me to assist her once she catches it, but I'm failing. The best I can do is to get her to follow me from one branch to another behind and above. She follows so silently that I had to put a bell on her leg to find her in the dense stand of trees. Even then, I sometimes have to close my eyes and concentrate to hear her location.

Murrundindi approached me after I had finished presenting the bird show at the zoo where we were both working. "I watched the show you just did. The birds share your respect for them. You're something very special," he said.

"The birds are well trained." I shook my head and blushed anyway.

"I heard that you are having some trouble connecting with the land."

I nodded and tried to look austere, angry that I felt like giving in to homesick tears. It was a small thing that should have merely befuddled, not crushed me.

"I can do something about that," he said and invited me to join him at the bush hut in the Coorinderk that night.

Murrundindi motions for me to join him in front of the fire. Turning my back to the warmth and facing his illuminated features I can see his expression is as warm as the fire, the face paint glowing with the flames. He touches a stone to the ground and speaks in words I can't understand but struggle to hear just the same.

I recognize the lilt of his voice, a calling to the earth. He presses a stone smooth from water and warm from touch to my forehead. I am dizzy from the smoke and reverberation, but am lifted to my toes and lightly returned to earth, a dancer reaching momentarily for the starlight.

I open my eyes, frightened a little by the rush of blood to my fingers and cheeks. Murrundindi smiles and says a few more staccato words. Then he speaks in English, "Did you feel anything?" I remain silent, uncertain.

"You did. I felt you lift all the way up." Murrundindi pauses and then says," You are already grounded." We stand with our eyes locked and my heart breaking. There is no helping me. I have all the tools I needed, I just can't use them. "There's something else though." Murrundindi places a friendly hand on my shoulder and bows to meet my eyes a little straighter. "I saw a man, an old man who has left you. Perhaps he has died?"

I chew on my lower lip and sigh. "My grandfather. He died less than a year ago." He had been the dreamtime master of my childhood, capturing my imagination with tales of wilds and falconry. He had become my hunting confidant as a young adult, listening carefully to my recounting of a perfect hunt and encouraging the respect and education gained from predator and prey. I do miss him.

"He is calling you back home. That is why you are not connecting." I must still look disappointed because he gives my shoulder a little squeeze. "I have an idea though. You must hunt barefoot."

"What?" There are three species of snake that live in the bush where I hunt. All three of them could kill me. The only armor I have is jeans and boots. I am about to call him certifiable when he commands, "Listen!" I move my chin with only the slightest sign of agreement, but he continues on. "Run your fingers through the earth and smear it on your face. Take off your shoes and allow the dirt between your toes. Listen. I mean really listen. Not just with your ears. Then walk with your hawk." He pats me one more time and turns away with a knowing smile. "Let me know how it goes."

I have to admit the idea of running through the bush barefoot and warrior-striped is ridiculous. I also have to admit I am going to do it anyway, but I don't need to confess this to anyone.

Fortunately Elektra distrusts other people even more than she distrusts me. If anyone joined the hunt, she headed for the next town over. So there is no one to criticize me when I tie the laces of my boots together and drape them around my neck. I wiggle my toes and fingers in the dirt with embarrassing glee and smear my face unabashedly. If I am bit by a tiger snake, so be it. At least I would be leaving Australia having given falconry my best shot.

My goshawk doesn't notice my dirty face and unshod feet. When I pull the hood from her head, she reviews the land and heads for a satisfactory perch without having given me a glance. I take a few careful steps and stop to listen. I hear rainbow lories above me, chattering while they tongue blossoms for taste and sustenance. I glance above me and spot them tumbling through the eucalypts like clowns. The next moment I think I hear the creaking-door sound of a gang-gang cockatoo. I might have, but it is interrupted by a butcher bird calling out its territory. In the distance I see something spreading a path through the tall ferns as it bounds away, probably a wallaby.

My goshawk is several paces in front of me now, waiting with impatience. I join her with less tender steps and our hunt begins in earnest. It is impossible not to notice my boots knocking against my chest, but I like the rhythm they are keeping and we make a steady pace. I begin to look ahead instead of surveying the ground directly below me. There are animals moving before us. I can see small signs of their wake. I have yet to see a rabbit, though, and wonder if the barefoot march is really a waste. Then I hear the didgeridoo.

It is odd to hear such a thing deep in the bush that edges on the vineyards of the wine country. Certainly there wouldn't be someone near by. The Wurundjeri have long since been rounded up and assimilated. The sound only lasted a moment anyway, so I dismiss it as imagination and move forward again. I take three steps when I hear the unmistakable hum again. This time I know where it is coming from, an old eucalyptus, living but bowing to the earth. I turn behind me to seek out my bird and find affirmation in her tense gaze. It is fixed on the same tree.

My heart beats just a little harder torn between wonder and skepticism, but I head for the tree, a prisoner of my curiosity. Maybe the wind blew through it just right or some animal is singing from its hollow. I am still contemplating the possibilities when at the base of the tree a rabbit springs from my feet.

I don't have time to yell "ho" to my bird, announcing the race. Elektra is already a wingbeat behind her quarry and then rolling with it through the ferns. I run to help and dive to restrain the kicking rabbit legs. On my belly I try to hold the rabbit and my own body still, casting my eyes down and praying that my goshawk will remain sure. When I finally raise my eyes her beak is dipped in blood. She gives me little notice and returns to her meal. I thank the rabbit and the didgeridoo, carefully jessing up my bird. Her jesses back in and tied to my glove, I sit up and enjoy the results of our first successful hunt.

I return to the flat I share, triumphant, but hold my tongue and the images in my mind. Rinsing my feet and face, I go to bed without a shower, too tired to bother with anything but dreams. In my sleep I dream of home.

I wake in the morning sneezing and coughing. In the bathroom I cough dirt into the sink and wash my face again, perplexed. I blow my nose in a soft wad of toilet paper and wonder at the dirt in my mucus. All morning I cough and sneeze and expel the earth.

My goshawk caught at least a dozen rabbits after that hunt. Sometimes I even knew where they were hiding before they broke for safety. I could hear the land. I miss Australia sometimes, but I like to think I brought back some of it with me.

I've been thinking a lot of Murrindindi and the grounding ceremony. I've thought about hunting barefoot, but the ceremony of it seemed wrong somehow. I have to be patient. I have to find my own way.

I've been avoiding the pond in La Quinta lately, the one I've now dubbed the fly-off pond. Anakin needs a simple hunt first;

I know that and so I'm waiting until we've mastered a language, an understanding before we go back and try again.

There's a circuit of twelve ponds I check in succession each morning and it's the sixth pond that seems the most hopeful to me, a pond centered in a field of alfalfa in Thermal. There are date palms to the south and desert saltbush scrub to the west. I sometimes stop in the morning to watch the sun rise in a rose glow through the short palms, while the Gambel's quail scuttle from their breakfast of fallen dates back to the impenetrable safety of the scrub.

I've been checking half-heartedly the last few days, but today what I see fills my heart and jumpstarts it. There's a single coot floating at its center.

I dip under the berm, jogging back to the truck bent at the waist so that the bird won't see the top of my head. Then I put the truck into reverse to give the coot even more room. I don't want it to accidentally flush. I need the bird to stay there until the falcon is in position.

I prep Anakin's telemetry and pull his braces with shaking hands. I'm muttering softly, "Don't fuck this up. Don't fuck this up." But I'm not talking to the falcon. I strike his braces and he takes to the sky.

He's gaining pitch fast and I wait to see if he'll center on the pond or fly away, pleading with him silently. This part is his job. I've done the first part of mine. I found him a slip and didn't screw it up before he could pin it. The peregrine does his part perfectly. He's seven hundred feet above the pond, waiting on.

I sprint for the pond, popping up on the berm screaming and clapping. I throw any rocks I can find. This pond is a third the size of the fly-off pond, but the coot won't budge. He paddles away from me, glancing at the sky. I look up to find

Anakin and blow the air out of my lungs. He's eight hundred feet now and focused on me. He's doing exactly what he needs to do and I'm not doing my part.

I throw one more rock, make sure the peregrine is still with me and then stop wasting time. I know what has to be done. I pull off my boots and vest, laying them on the shore. Then I take off my sweatshirt too so that there might be something dry left to wear and wade into the pond.

There's been a hard frost for the last few nights and it's cold enough to see my breath, but I don't notice that the water is cold. In three steps, though, I'm up to my chest. The pond is deeper than I thought. I splutter and tread water, checking for the falcon. He's still waiting on so I stretch forward, moving for the coot.

A coot looks a lot like a duck, but it's different. The bird is more chicken than duck, a member of the rail family. So when he finally decides that pressure is too much, his exit isn't graceful. His wings stutter against the surface of the pond and for a few steps he's clown-walking across the water. Then he's in the air, off the reservoir and crossing the alfalfa.

"Ho ho ho!" I'm screaming loud enough to reach the sky, sputtering through the water lapping between my open lips, but I don't need to call. The falcon is already tucked into a dive and slamming his quarry into the ground.

CHAPTER FOUR

Worshipping Ducks

"You swam?" Tom Austin asks me over the phone. He sounds disapproving, but I know better.

"Yes, but we caught a coot," I say.

"You need a dog," he says. "Don't let him catch many more coots. They're too easy. Let me know when you catch a duck." He hangs up the phone.

I think to myself that I might catch a cold first, but that I just might have the hang of this. I'm starting to see ducks in the ponds and the peregrine is starting to believe in me. We catch two more coots and then I'm ready to give the fly-off pond another try.

"How long has it been since he's flown off?" my mom asks. I can hear the sewing machine whirring in the background of our phone call. My apartment is silent. Anakin is sleeping on his screen perch and the African grey is fluffed, his head bobbing with the weight of his sleepiness.

"Nearly a month, but don't jinx me," I say. "Anything from Clyde?" I ask because she hasn't said a thing about him in weeks. My sisters told him to leave her alone and let her get on with her life. I doubt he understood, but I'm sure they meant that they wanted him to let them get on with their lives as well.

I feel so sorry for my half-siblings and guilty for the relief of not having to be involved.

"Haven't heard a peep," she says. "You know, I've finished three quilts this month. Maybe I should start on a new book proposal."

"You should," I say. Then we wrap up our conversation because my mom wants to focus on her work and I want to get some sleep.

The fly-off pond is holding two coots, six mallards and ten gadwall. The mallards are much too big for him. They are not only three times his size, but they're willful fighters. They are the most common and easily tamed of the city ducks, but there is much to admire about the mallard. It's only their commonality that encourages people to ignore the blazing colors of the drakes. "Green-heads," we call them, giving the name the emphasis of a jewel. They are beautiful ducks and I don't want him to catch one. If he tries and the ensuing battle is brutal, the little falcon may give up on ducks for good. So I'm counting on the mallards leaving the pond first. I'll flush them when he's out of position and then push the gadwall. I'm getting better at bullying ducks off the water.

Anakin is in a race these days to rise into an adequate pitch. He doesn't wander or waste time. He never loses sight of me and trusts that I will do my part if he gets into position.

We've lost a lot of ducks, of course. He is a baby bird and there are many things to learn the hard way. I don't mind because the waterfowl that have mastered the means of falcon evasion are just as admirable to watch. I witness moments of survival every day that are just shy of a miracle, but happen so fast it's impossible to tell the difference.

Anakin surveys his surroundings when I pull the hood. I think I'm coming to understand the subtle expression in his feathers and see recognition on his face. He knows this place and I'm hoping that familiarity doesn't breed contempt. I hope that he doesn't automatically fly away. Many falconers think that a bird who has learned to fly off from a place will repeat the behavior time and time again. I am certain that it's all a matter of their belief system. Does he believe he can catch duck here? Does he believe in me?

Anakin paddles his wings and looks to the sky, maybe seeing the subtle changes of jet streams and thermals, maybe looking for the balloon. I'll never know, but will surely get better at guessing as time goes on. The falcon launches toward the rising sun in the east and I cross my fingers that he will return and fly high.

These hunts happen so fast now. He's nearly in position in four minutes and already it's time for me to get to work. He's high enough to pin the ducks, but just far enough out of position that I should be able to get the mallards off without incident. They always come off fearlessly and immediately.

Today is different. There must be something in the falcon's wingbeat that I cannot see. I am beginning to discover that the ducks know when the falcon means business and when he is just thinking it over. The waterfowl seem to gamble based on odds that they can read better than I can. Today, the mallards don't want to leave. So by the time I finally convince them with my new slingshot and pocket full of glass marbles, the falcon is in perfect position.

Tom told me that it takes confidence and experience for a falcon to be willing to dive through a flock of ducks. The peregrine has to be decisive and sure-footed. That's why you start with a single coot, an easy decision that even clumsy talons can manage. The flock of eight ducks that rises off the water is a new test. Surely it's too much to ask.

All the same, Anakin makes a fast decision and dives. I press my hand to my mouth when I see the green-headed duck tumble and hear the familiar quack. Then I sprint in the hopes of getting there fast enough to save my falcon a beating.

The rolling chaparral is tough hunting. Sadie has learned to soar above and wait for a flush, which is tough to come by. There are plenty of cottontails and jackrabbits out there, but they are very hard to produce, especially the jacks. We have yet to catch a jack out here in our own backyard. Still, I am determined.

I skipped out of work today to get home and hunt. There is only an hour or so left of the light, so I throw open the door to the mews and immediately start my trudge through the chaparral. Sadie is set above me, calling the whole way. After an hour we aren't seeing much of anything and the sun is getting lower. Disappointed, I start to make my way back to the mews. It is always these moments of defeat that produce. A jack bursts from my feet and crests the hill in front of me before I even think to yell.

The jack and my stooping red-tail disappear from my sight. Racing up the hill, stumbling and yelling I reach the hilltop in time to see the end of what must have been a spectacular chase. Sadie has grabbed the jack, but doesn't have a firm grasp on it. The huge hare four times her weight is taking her for a ride and is going to scrape her off if I don't get there.

I am racing through the sagebrush which crackles beneath my boots, desperate to get to my hawk before we lose our first "back forty" jack.

The hare is just slipping from her feet when I dive for the back legs, sliding across the coarse soil, my momentum taking us another fifteen feet down the hill. For all my efforts, Sadie just gives me a dirty look, almond-shaped eyes and raised hackles. It's okay, I know it was me that tipped the scale. I thank the jack for its life and end the battle.

I position her meal in front of her, but the exertion has caught up with Sadie and we both sit panting. Standing up, I wipe the sweat from my forehead, exhausted but jubilant. This is when I hear the clapping and yelling.

In my second season with my Sadie, my grandfather's health is failing and we are both living with my father. Our house is perched at the edge of several hundred acres of land. My grandfather isn't getting around well, but he would sometimes set up a lawn chair on the driveway and watch the hunt progress. Down below me at the house, my grandfather is standing on his chair, applauding and cheering.

I reach the falcon and the duck panting, my side twisting into a knot of pain and find that I could have strolled over. There is no battle. It is as if the duck has willingly sacrificed his life to have the honor of being a great warrior's first kill. I check to make sure the drake mallard has left us and is no longer suffering and then tuck my head between my knees, weeping. The falcon doesn't notice my jagged breathing, he doesn't understand that catching a drake mallard is impossible for a falcon his size and that it is his first duck.

I have never eaten duck, but I thought I should eat this one. I could put it the freezer for Anakin to eat the rest later, but I thought that I should honor it too. If I can figure out how to cook it.

With the mallard in my sink and the falcon on the patio, crop full and bathing, I examine my task. This isn't easy, cleaning a duck. I love birds. To take one apart with my hands and a carving knife makes my throat tighten. I tell myself to suck it up, but I can't. I separate the skin on the breast, slip the knife underneath and wipe at the tears on my right cheek with my right shoulder.

This is sustenance, I tell myself. This is survival. This is how chickens, pigs, and cows are prepped for your table while you look away. The difference is you know this duck. The difference is you honor this duck with your carving knife and skillet, with your tears.

I peel the fatty skin away from the breast and with as much precision as I can muster in a first attempt, separate the breast muscle from the bone. The breast is still warm and the bruises from the falcon's talons are evident in deeper ebbs of red. The flesh reads like a story. In my hands is the tale of a successful hunt. I slide the meat into a bowl of olive oil, rice wine vinegar, and spices, slipping it into the refrigerator to marinate for the rest of the day. The wings and legs are saved for Anakin.

For dinner I lay the breast meat into a skillet snapping with olive oil and cook it medium rare. I serve myself duck meat with a salad of baby greens and a thirty-dollar bottle of cabernet sauvignon. I choose to sit in a chair with a good view of the falcon. The room is lit by a white pillar candle at my table and he looks gorgeous and sleepy in the flickering light.

The duck meat is a surprise. It tastes like a fine cut of steak without the texture of beef. It doesn't need much chewing, dissolving into pure taste between my teeth. The duck is so rich, that what the falcon left for me is the perfect-sized meal. I sip the wine and marvel over the best meal I have ever eaten. Then I raise my glass to honor the duck and again to honor the falcon. I know the falcon cannot understand my words, but some deep urge in my storyteller's heart has me recounting the tale of a young peregrine's first duck. I can't help but imagine my grandfather listening.

CHAPTER FIVE

Not a Hunter

The falcon shoots across the sky, away from me, away from the pond, and is gone. The signal of his transmitter promises that he is nearby, but nearby becomes somewhere in the salt scrub brush and tamarisk. I would have done better with a machete, but I do my best beating back the tangle of stubborn desert growth with my arms and heavy boots.

There must have been something too tempting to forgo for the falcon to choose this ten-foot-high wilderness as a place to take down game. I know it can't be a duck. I hadn't flushed the pond yet. I imagine dove, pigeon, maybe even a crow, until I get close enough to spot the feathers. I gasp hard and then choke on the dusty fallout of my brush beating.

Kneeling to pick up a primary feather, I bite my lip. It belongs to a falcon. I pick up another primary and a secondary. Together they are the beginnings of a wing. Holding them together I become calmer. They are falcon feathers, but the wing is too small to belong to a peregrine.

Turning off the receiver, I follow the trail of feathers. They are rust, blue, brown and scattered recklessly. Further up a stand of tamarisk, feathers are still fluttering down in a slow sway as if riding a breeze. I wonder what has killed this falcon until I hear the ching ching of a brass acorn bell and there is little question.

I part the wispy branches of the salt cedar to reveal Anakin with his meal. Most of the breast is gone, but there is no mistaking the quarry. It was a male kestrel, a falcon, although smaller. I look away for a moment, disgusted, ashamed, wondering what part I played in this. Then look into Anakin's face and see nothing to compare to my emotions. I don't even see hunger.

I push away my human sentiments and gently lift my own falcon out of his secluded dining spot. At least he had the sense to hide himself away from another bigger predator. I let him finish his meal because I don't know what else to do.

I wonder what the flight looked like. If he could overtake his own brethren, surely he could outfly a mere dove. I shake off the thoughts, giving him more food from my pocket, slipping the hood on his head.

I cannot take the kestrel with me. They are not legal to hunt. A falconer's only protection from a falcon balking regulations is the "leave it lay" law. I can't be caught with a dead raptor in my vest, so I tuck the tiercel kestrel gently at the base of the bushes, the tamarisk a tasseled tomb. We'll try for more suitable quarry tomorrow.

Easier to think about the law than that I'm not ashamed at all.

Yesterday's hunt forgotten, today's hunt was well flown, but the coot was disappointing. There was no contest, no chance. I hadn't meant to flush such easy quarry, but the commotion of the wily shovelers, small and quick-winged ducks also swimming on the pond, urged the coot into panic. Six times the shovelers made my falcon look the fool as they dipped and swung around the edge of the pond, evading their flying pursuer. Despite the ducks' ludicrous spoon of a bill and clown-painted feathers, wingbeat for wingbeat, it was the falcon that was the jester. In the peregrine's frustration, the coot lumbering low across the salt flats must have been more than any hungry predator could resist. If I were wing-shooting, I wouldn't have taken the shot, but then, I'm not the hunter. I'm the caddy, the assistant, some mornings the Irish setter. I do my job. The choice was made. We could come back to the edge of the Salton Sea and chase shovelers again.

I think most falconers are hunters, so my inadequacy has nothing to do with my choice of weapons. I remember a hunt during my two-year apprenticeship when one of the falconers displaced his hawk as star hunter. The Harris' hawk that was supposed to be chasing the rabbits we pushed up from vineyards had other plans for his day. He dropped from the sky to clutch at dirt clods and scurry after lizards like an ill-equipped roadrunner. The falconer continued to search for rabbits, despite his hawk's lack of interest. Personally, I was bored, at least until the falconer pounced. His body stretched into a tackle, ending with a fall that pounded the dust from the ground. He remained prone, but a jack rabbit screamed in his palms. Now the hawk was rabid, but the falconer clung to the hare and pushed away the crabbing hawk. With the same fluidity he had swept the jack from its scrape, he slipped it into his vest, crying victory.

He would let the rabbit go later when the hawk was out of sight. For now the hare kicking inside his vest was the spoils of a successful hunt and it didn't matter who caught it. I will never catch a rabbit with my hands. I ignored the hawk and followed the falconer for the rest of the hunt, squinting for hidden hares I might point out to him.

It's always been like this. When I was eight I found a praying mantis perched outside on the cat's dish. Flies were zipping in to lap at the remnants of canned food. The mantis flashed with worshipful precision and then held one between her bent legs. I watched her nibble the fly's head away, and when she had completed her meal, waited patiently for the next strike. The next attack was a near-miss and I had no choice but to help. Assistance came in the form of a flyswatter. I stunned a fly and held it buzzing between my fingers in front of the pale and graceful insect. She turned her head left and right, and then tilted it up to look at me. Hard to say what she saw exactly, but eventually she only saw the fly and snatched it from my fingers. I fed her six more like this before she began to ignore me and clean her face like a cat, both of us full.

Predator worship is an odd thing, but perhaps not so odd for a woman. I am aware that I am more prey than predator. Last night I dreamt I was tracking my falcon through a forest, following the breadcrumb beeps of his transmitter. A shrieking rose from the shadow-drenched pines behind me and pierced my heart. It was a cry that resonated through my muscles, like a woman raising her voice against torture, but it wasn't human. I've only read of mountain lions making such a sound, but this sort of straight fact isn't important in a dream. I was in terrible danger and had no choice but to wake up. Even with my eyes opened, my chest burned and my muscles ached. I knew there was no mountain lion in my house, but I am no stranger to being stalked.

I wake like this frequently, although the mountain lion dream was a first. There is no point in trying to sleep again. I only return to the fear. Instead I must listen, smell, taste the air and then pace until my twitchy prey senses ebb away. I depend on these senses. I've earned them.

When I was twenty-three I was stalked by a man who lived in the condo next door. He would knock on my bedroom window in the middle of the night or ring my doorbell and run away. This seemed more like a nuisance than a danger, until he nearly murdered my younger brother on my living room couch.

I had gone to the office for an hour and the man walked into my apartment unannounced, like a lover quietly letting himself in. When he saw the other man in my home he left, but returned armed, perhaps to kill the invader to his territory. A gun to his head, my brother stared into the face of my stalker until he proved he was unflinching. The man lowered his gun, a gun we would find out later was loaded, a round chambered, but a gun that remained unfired when the burglar retreated.

My stalker went to jail. I'm safe now, but I still own that couch and sometimes on nights like this I stare at the bloodstain that was nearly there. I know now the stalker watched me sleep at night; let himself into my home to be near and imagine. I remember sometimes waking to a strange stillness and finding my apartment lit, the front door open and pondering my own carelessness. Now I can imagine my stalker's heartbeat quicken at the click and swing of an unlocked door and his red curly head backlit by the light he left on in my kitchen—all of these details that had escaped my notice. I know full well I could be snatched like a jack rabbit from my scrape, but perhaps my intimacy with the hunter is honing my senses and keeping me safe.

Back out in the field I give Anakin another chance at the shovelers. His budding prowess as a hunter is spellbinding. I believe now that he could survive as a wild falcon without me. I watch him learn lessons and perfect his aerobatics on a daily basis. He will remember how the ducks got away and it will be gorgeous to watch. I will swim if I have to—whatever it takes to facilitate the hunt.

When I pull up to the pond my excitement ignites into anger. There are two men walking down the berm, one holding the carcass of a duck, the other leading a chocolate Labrador. I roll down my window and yell at them.

"Is that the drake shoveler that was on this pond?"

"What?"

"Wait, I'm coming over." I storm to the men whose faces wear the shellac mask a hunter puts on when approached by an animal rights activist. I am no activist, but I know the pond is too close to the road for a shotgun and I know they have to be jump shooters, a sloppy, lazy faction of duck hunters. More importantly I know they have shot my duck. "Did you shoot that shoveler off this pond?"

"Yep."

"Bastards." I pause to give the limp duck a disappointed glance. "I was going to fly my falcon at them."

Their faces lose their shellac and open to astonishment. I square off at them, my fists on my hips and sigh when they start laughing.

"I wondered why you knew what a shoveler was."

Suddenly I have been elevated to something of an equal and the men give me easy smiles and directions to a couple of ponds I might fly. I scrub the neck of their Lab with my fingernails and smile back uncertainly.

Their truck is bigger than mine, four-wheel drive with mud splashed across its sides. Their Lab is loaded into a kennel in the back and as I watch them pull their camouflaged legs into the cab, there is no mistaking them as anything but hunters. I look down at my simple jeans and grey sweatshirt, my boots just barely dipped in the grey mud of the salt flats and think I look more like a bird watcher.

I follow their directions and find another pond, buried in the desert-fringed vineyards. Anakin is outdone by ringbills this time and two hours later I am scouting the water of my last few favorite ponds. I shouldn't have been surprised to find the jump shooters again.

"We feel really bad about shooting your spoonbill."

"Me too." I say, thinking they aren't so much sorry as amused.

"Any luck?"

"No. You?"

"Shot three more ducks, gadwall," the hunter answers and then notes my silence. "If there's a duck here we'll let you fly it." But there isn't. They offer to let me follow them for the rest of their hunt, help if I want and take their scraps. I follow them to the first two ponds and then turn for home without saying goodbye.

Most duck hunters hide in blinds, battle the water and the weather. They take great pains to perfect their silence and camouflage. They spend their spare moments carving realistic decoys and learning to speak the language of ducks. When the ducks fly in enticed by the hunter's glamoured waters there is pleasure in that as much as the kill. If the hunter is lucky he even makes a few shots. It's an art form. No love of mine, but an art form just the same.

The jump shooters drive around finding ducks in small ponds, push them off and then shoot them as they leave. No contest. My jump shooters are well on their way to shooting more ducks on Sunday than my falcon has caught in the three months of the season. That shoveler would have had a damn good chance of getting away beneath my falcon. I wish he had been given it.

Perhaps it is natural for some men to kill without regard to style or end result. Shovelers are terrible eating. Those men were skeet shooting and the ducks may as well have been clay pigeons shot in the back. Between the two of us, my falcon and I eat everything we catch. Anakin hunts for food, not numbers. *That* seems natural.

Hemingway hunted for trophies too, but mainly everything he killed was eaten by himself or by the hunting party. Hemingway, however, took pride in killing my precious predators. He admittedly shot hyenas in the gut simply because he hated them. Then again, like me, Papa understood that he, too, was prey. He knew a glancing shot from a panicked hunter was a dangerous thing in a lion hunt. The cat would turn, enraged, his normal brute strength now a conflagration of wild ire. Someone better have a smooth shot with deadly aim or the hunter would be reduced to ribbons and left as some other animal's meal.

I would never kill a predator for sport, but watched helplessly when Anakin killed the kestrel, forgiving him instantly. Food is food when you're hungry, but I also know that Anakin wasn't very hungry when he killed the kestrel. Nestled in the tamarisk and clutching his prey I could see that he had done it for sport. I still forgave him. In fact, I was proud—his triumph a guilty contagion.

Maybe I'm wrong. Given the choice I would be the predator. Maybe I'm a hunter after all.

CHAPTER SIX

Whitewater

"Are you hunting my ducks?" asks the lanky man with the craggy face and the handlebar mustache complete with long beard. The wind rising up from Palm Springs to the east whips my hair into my face and I pull a strand away from my mouth, pausing before I answer.

This place is fenced in, but it is ideal for Anakin. There are three small ponds and all three held ringbill ducks, small waterfowl perfectly matched to a small peregrine. The ranch is a surprise oasis tucked next to Whitewater River. I suspect that the waterfowl have used it as a respite on the desert length of the flyway for a hundred years or more.

I saw the rancher driving his red Ford pickup and thought I should take my chances and try to get his blessing to come on the property. I had met him at the gate, asking permission to fly my falcon but hadn't expected him to ask if the falcon would be killing his ducks. He didn't sound happy about it either. I didn't know what the right answer was, but knew there was only one true one.

"Yes, my falcon hunts ducks." I look into his eyes to see if they have hardened, but there is no change in his expression, so I continue. "Come look at him. He's just a little male peregrine. He's working so hard and there aren't very many places with small ducks where he can hunt." The man follows me to my truck and sighs when he sees Anakin. I haven't made a dent in his gruff exterior but my peregrine has made him smile.

"I used to have sparrow hawks," he admits to me. "That was years ago." He looks up into the sky as if the tiny falcons he flew as a boy might still be following over his head. "You can fly him here," he says. Then he tells me that he won't let any gun hunters on the property. He explains that he loves the ducks on his ponds, raises orphan ducklings in the spring. "But you can fly your falcon here. It won't hurt nothin'." He is an old cattle rancher and every rancher agrees to lose a few of their stock to the predators. My falcon isn't a threat. As far as the rancher was concerned, the falcon belongs there.

We shake hands, exchange names and then Butch takes a long look at my chest and nods. Patches of wet are showing through my sweatshirt from my soaked bra underneath. I have already been swimming in his pond, flushing ringbills for Anakin, but Butch hadn't caught me on his property. He doesn't say anything about my wet clothes, but I understand the nod. He means that it is good thing I asked, because even though I am a woman, he would have kicked my ass off his land for good if he had caught me trespassing. In Texas you would get shot for such a breach of civility. I should be glad we are in California. I squirm for a few more moments under Butch's gaze and then he smiles.

"I'll come out and help you flush ducks if I see you out there," Butch says, touching the rim of an invisible cowboy hat. I smile and almost curtsy, already imagining a long friendship built on seasons of successful hunts.

The next morning, Butch finds me walking to the pond. Anakin is already in the air, close to a thousand feet high. I explain to

Butch that he and I should flank the pond and how the ducks won't come off without coercion when there is a serious falcon waiting on above. Ducks know what danger looks like. I glanced up into the sky and watch my falcon hit the good air, the place above a thousand feet where it suddenly becomes easier to fly. His wingbeat becomes a quick snap and I hurry to get to the other side of the pond. "Okay, Butch, let's go!"

Butch has found a stick and a piece of plywood that he is beating like a drum. I nod in approval, throwing rocks in the water and yelling. The ducks are pushing to the end of the pond away from us and we almost have them pinched off.

I look up to find Anakin and don't see him. "Where is he?" Butch points and I squint into that piece of sky. I see nothing, then move my eyes higher and gasp.

Anakin is a tiny flashing speck no less than fifteen hundred feet and still climbing. The sight makes my heart constrict. He looks like he could easily sky out, disappearing forever and I wondered even after all we've been through how I can hope to maintain a connection with a falcon that is so very high. My hand twitches for the lure to call him down, get him back safely to me, but I glance at Butch who stands serene, his faith in the falcon unquestionable. So instead I pull a marble out of my pocket and load my slingshot. I shoot the marble into the flock of ducks, give them a final push. Butch and I yell together, running at the waterfowl with menace and watch them all lift off in unison.

Anakin is waiting, wings set, trying to decide when to stoop. Then he commits to the fall and I yell to Butch, "Here he comes!" I start to shout "ho," call that game is in the air, but the sight of my bird leaves me speechless. From fifteen hundred feet he is coming straight down. His body is shaped like a missile, no resistance, full speed. It is not a shape I have ever seen his body morph into before. He has never had a decisive stoop from that high.

I had seen that shape before in the sky diving video of a biologist, Ken Franklin and his peregrine, Frightful. As Ken dropped in freefall, shooting video, his peregrine passed him, tucked in a stoop clocked at 180 miles per hour. This tuck and fall was pure committed peregrine and a vision that will be etched in my memory for the rest of my falconry career. It was a falcon defying the air, redefining terminal velocity and now I was a witness to this amazing feat of peregrine evolution.

All the same, fifteen hundred feet is not necessarily a realistic pitch to hunt ducks from and by the time Anakin makes it to the moving flock, they are hugging the water again and he misses. And once he misses, the ducks make a hasty getaway. Anakin gives them chase, but by then the ringbill ducks are at full speed. The falcon has no chance of catching them. The waterfowl are gone. There is nothing left to do but fly him to the lure.

Anakin arrives ready for another chance. He is at seven hundred feet, remounted and waiting for us to flush something else, despite the absence of waterfowl. Yet he doesn't hesitate when I pull the lure from my vest; again he drops at full speed. My heart pounds because I don't think I'll manage this timing. The falcon is coming too fast, but I keep swinging the lure. "Oh no you don't," I say and forget that Butch is watching. There is nothing but a sky-cutting peregrine and a leather pouch singing through the air. There is no one but me and Anakin.

The falcon coming in as fast as he's ever flown at me and yet I'm seeing the motions delineated like dance steps. Serve the lure now. Pull it. Turn. The falcon rips by me, looking over his shoulder. "Ha!" I yell. And he flips over, rolling back toward me. His feet almost have the lure and then I'm speeding it out of his path.

This time the falcon only takes a glance over his shoulder. He's got a better plan, I can tell. He wings purposefully west, disappearing behind a stand of cottonwood trees and now I have no idea where he'll be coming from next. I swing the lure and scan the sky, the ground, the trees. My heart is pounding and I'm suppressing a giggle.

Butch is standing closer now, between me and the cottonwoods. He's smiling, but I'm too focused on finding my stealthy falcon to smile back. Then I see him, clipping the five-foot creosote, he's been using them as cover and he's almost to me. I barely manage to pull the lure in time. The falcon rolls again, turns back and clips the top of Butch's white head as he speeds straight for me.

"Whoo-hoo!" Butch yells and raises a fist. I pivot for Anakin to make one more pass and then whistle that the lure is his. The peregrine flutters to the ground panting and glaring. Butch and I share another smile, but don't speak. We both spend a moment looking into the sky, at the stand of cottonwoods, and I wonder if he's reliving the flight as well.

Butch stays to watch Anakin eat a starling pulled from my pocket and tells me a little about his life. Butch's family had a duck hunting club years ago in Los Banos, an area that's a favorite falconer's haunt in California. He was a rock climber too. He took a 120-foot-fall and broke every bone on the left side of his body. He is still not fully recovered and can't work a regular job. He was offered a position managing the cattle and now tends eighty head of beef cattle at Whitewater Ranch.

It looks like a peaceful job and Butch seemed like a peaceful man and definitely the sort you want helping you hunt. I was amazed he could point out my high-flying peregrine. I've flown with falconers that can't make out the little black tiercel when he's half as high. I was just sorry he hadn't seen a successful hunt.

Butch shakes his head at me, "Nah, I was just happy to see the little guy fly." And he gives me a ride back to the gate.

"I hope I can fly here for a long time," I say.

"Me too," Butch calls over his shoulder and he leaves me at the gate.

Butch and I hunt ringbill three days later and this time Anakin catches one. While we watch the peregrine feast and the sun stretch higher to the east, Butch tells me stories about White-water Ranch.

"This place has been here since the 1850s," he says.

"Has it always been a cattle ranch?" I ask.

"Always," Butch says. "But it's also been a stagecoach stop and a railway depot." He sounds proud and I know he loves this place. I look around and wonder why no one realizes it's here.

Butch tells me about the crazy Talmadge brothers and their cattle runs from here at the floor of the desert up to Big Bear in the mountains every summer. They were wild boys that liked their fun. They had plenty of problems running a ranch and deserved to raise a little hell from time to time.

Whitewater Ranch has always been beautiful, but never easy. The grizzlies used to lumber down from the mountains for a meal and even the antelope caused problems with the cattle and the ranch.

"Grizzlies? Antelope?" I say, trying to imagine those long-gone animals running this ground, drinking from this pond. Butch assures me that he isn't pulling my leg, but that it's really the people that have caused problems for the ranch.

He spins a tale about the manhunt for Willie Boy and how it had ended in a standoff right here in this ranch. He points to a cottonwood where a cattle rustler had been hung.

"Who owns it now?" I ask.

"It's BLM land," he answers. Then tells me about the Stockers, he thinks one of the final owners of the property. James Stocker was the last cowboy lawman in Southern California, the last sheriff with a real posse. I find myself imagining Whitewater as a place that will outlast every person who has ever loved it. In a place with as little known history as California, Whitewater seemed as immortal as its phantom past.

"This is an amazing place," I say, more to myself than to Butch.

"Enjoy it while it lasts," he says.

Chapter Seven

Sometimes It's Worth Losing

Sis Jackson has convinced me to bring Anakin out to the La Quinta Country Club. Sis is a volunteer and board member of the Living Desert where I work and a more importantly a friend. She is a fan of wildlife. So I want her to see the falcon fly. It wouldn't hurt to do the country club a favor either. I have discovered that golf courses don't really care for ducks. Herds of grass-grazing waterfowl manage to make a slimy mess of the greens. However, the folks that own the high-end houses edging the course weren't going to let the groundskeepers shoot any ducks and certainly didn't care for the booming cannons that had been used to scare the waterfowl away. The idea of shooing the offending birds away with a falcon was appealing.

I had checked out the course yesterday, met Sis in the parking lot. We procured a golf cart to take a look. I whistled when I saw the big pond at the start of the course. There were no less than one hundred widgeon on the pond, a good twenty ringbills and a handful of mallards. We investigated two smaller ponds, they too had a handful of ducks, but weren't as open and falcon-friendly. So we went back to the big pond and I strategized for the next morning, but wasn't liking what I came up with.

The pond was just too big. More than two Olympic-sized swimmings pools, there was ample room for the ducks to just swim around me, even if I decided I needed to get in the water. I needed a dog. Sis waved at passing golfers as I stood and contemplated and a woman stopped to chat. Sis told her why I was there and introduced me. Debbie was excited to hear I would be replacing the cannons; she had a rescued German shorthaired pointer that was terrified of echoing booms.

"A GSP?" I asked. "Does she like the water?"

Debbie told me that the dog didn't like the water much at all but her other two GSPs did. Then she shook my hand, wished me luck and left before I had a chance to angle for a borrowed dog.

Sis smiled, "That's Andy Williams' wife."

"Really? The singer?" I asked. Only in the desert where fame meets manufactured wilderness, I thought, and worried over how I would get the ducks off without annoying the local celebrities. Sis said she would be there in the morning and Don, one of the groundskeepers, was happy to assist by throwing golf balls as well. I was still not convinced that I could make it work, but grudgingly agreed to come back at six thirty in the morning with my falcon.

I dreamt about the pond all night. I swam with with the ducks and couldn't get them off. I lost my bird in the new tighter terrain. I chased widgeon across the greens in wet jeans and never got anything to flush beneath my bird. I worried after waterfowl all night long and woke exhausted.

Now I only have an hour and a half of early light before the golfers begin putting, but I glance at the pond still full of widgeon and coots and nod. Maybe it is open enough and there are enough ducks that we can manage a hunt. So Anakin and I are chauffeured by Don. He is tall and smiling beneath a mop of curly brown hair and only a few years older than me. He drives us onto the greens in the golf cart, Sis riding along with us.

When I pull the hood, the falcon looks around him for a long while, unsure of the new scenery, but eventually he launches off the glove and begins to climb above the pond.

Don and I take the opposite sides of the pond and I instruct him on how to flush the ducks, yelling instructions across the pond. We are both running along the shore, a smattering of marbles flung from my slingshot and Don's golf balls are peppering the water around the ducks. Six widgeon rise and clear the water, crossing the greens.

Anakin comes down in a tight stoop, but instead of hitting a duck, falls behind his target and then chases it out of our sight. I shake my head. "Baby bird move," I say and wait for him to come back. He knows better than that, but this terrain is something different for him. He remounts at the same height and we flush again and again. Anakin falls behind a duck instead of hitting it and then remounts. It's the widgeon, I think. The flock wheels and twists, hugging the edge of the pond, confusing the falcon and then splashing back down. The falcon doesn't know what to do.

I wait on the falcon for a while, trying to decide how to flush the remaining ducks. I am just yelling at Don to push the other end of the pond when a renegade hen pushes off the water and begins to make tight circles above the pond. I ignore her until I see my falcon streaking across the sky from the corner of my eye. What is he doing? He barrels in and binds to the brown duck in a tangle of feathers only one hundred feet above the water, muscling her to the ground.

That is not how you catch a duck, I murmur to myself and sprint, getting to them just as they hit the ground. I hear a chorus of cheers from the onlookers, but am too busy to look up and smile. I'm reaching in to save my falcon who is getting kicked and bounced by a hen gadwall. She must have been the only gadwall in the bunch, but a species my frustrated falcon understood. So he did what he felt needed to be done.

It definitely wasn't fine falconry, but I am proud of him. He's determined and strong. I let him enjoy his duck and I look after his feathers as he eats, making sure he is sitting tight and not mashing his tail. But his tail doesn't look quite right. Where is the transmitter? I reached down to feel for the barrel shape of metal clipped to the central feather of his tail, but I don't feel anything. Where is his deck feather? The transmitter and the feather are gone.

I track the transmitter to the pond where it lays in the shallow edge still attached to the feather the duck ripped out. Don fishes it out of the water for me and I turn it over in my hand a little forlorn.

Twelve feathers in the train of a falcon. Anakin now has eleven. They can manage with one deck feather missing, a small hole in the fan of tail feathers. A bigger hole and his brakes won't work as well. I'll just have to make sure he never loses another. No more transmitters on the tail. Sometimes the feathers grow back. It depends on whether or not the follicle has been damaged. Looking at the bloody tip of the plucked feather, I think there is probably too much trauma. I'm certain this feather will never grow back, a visible scar on a warrior.

Don drives me back to my truck, expressing his amazement at how such a small falcon could take down such a large duck. Sis is impressed by the flight as well, but no one seems to notice I haven't put a dent in the armada of ducks that has resettled on the pond. They are both hoping that I'll be back with the falcon to try again. I smile and nod, tuck the falcon away on his perch in the truck. I could come back, but I'm imagining the clean stretch of sky above Whitewater and the solitude.

I wake in the middle of the night with an intense pain radiating across my belly. I make it to the bathroom to vomit and then the agony becomes too debilitating to pick up the phone and call for help. I don't remember falling asleep, so I likely passed out. Either way, I wake on the bathroom floor to the sound of falconry bells. I have to get up and fly my bird.

The worst of the throbbing through my gut is gone. Maybe it was food poisoning or an embarrassingly painful bout of gas. When I get up, though, I find I can only hobble to the screen perch. I feel like someone kicked me in my right side.

Your appendix is in your right side, I think to myself. Then I remind myself that I hate doctors. If I go to the doctor they will most likely confirm that yes, indeed, it was just gas. I hate being called a hypochondriac even more than I dislike physicians. All the same, there are only six more weeks until I turn thirty-three. People die from burst appendixes. So I get dressed and limp to the urgent care facility.

It isn't until late in the afternoon that I get sent to the emergency room. At this point, I'm hungry, I'm tired, and my right side doesn't hurt anymore. At least, not until the doctor jabs his finger into it. "Ouch," I say when he asks if it hurts. Then I say, "Only a little." He's looking at my chart and reading the results of my MRI.

"I'm scheduling you for an emergency appendectomy," he says. And I think to myself that I drove myself to the emergency room and don't want to leave my truck, that somebody needs to feed the falcon and the African grey and that anyway, he's wrong.

"Can I go home for a little while first?" I ask. "I'll come back," I add when he frowns.

"Your appendix is going to burst," he says.

"I feel fine," I say. "I'll come back."

"People die from their appendix bursting," he says. "I have no idea why you aren't in tremendous pain, but it is going to burst. The surgeon will be here in two hours." He pats me on the shoulder. "Get some rest."

I wake with the surgeon standing over my bed.

"How do you feel?" he asks because I am now missing the little organ that was threatening to kill me. I blink. I feel surprisingly well and nod. "That's a really cool tattoo you have," he says.

I blink again, imagining my surgeon and the nurses discussing the blaze of my tattoo across my pale skin. I am too tired to feel violated.

"What kind of bird is it?" asks the surgeon.

"A phoenix," I mumble, imagining the lick of flames across my right hip.

"Up from the ashes," he muses and I don't respond.

"How long until . . ." I mumble instead.

"You'll be back at it in two weeks," he says, all business and no smile.

Ten days, I bargain silently because he doesn't really know what I was asking. I fall back asleep before he leaves the room. They release me that same afternoon.

"Are you sure you don't want me to come?" my mom asks.

"I'm walking," I say. "I just have to take it easy for a week. No need for a babysitter."

"I know, but . . ." She trails off and I understand what she's saying, but it isn't necessary.

"I'm fine, really. And nobody should have to be around me until I can fly my falcon again." My mom laughs because she knows that I'm grumpy about losing two weeks of the season. We had just found a rhythm and there will only be a few weeks left when I can stand steady in the field again.

"You'll be back out there in no time. Just be careful," she says. Then she pauses. "I know I've said this before, but I'm so sorry I wasn't there for you those years when you were a little girl. I should never have left you like that."

"And I've said this before too. You were just a baby, Mom." I say this because she was only twenty-two when she left. She *was* just a baby.

"Someday you're going to have to get angry," she says and I laugh. "Why are you laughing?" She honestly doesn't know. So I tell her not to worry about it and to let me get some sleep so I can heal faster.

While I sleep I dream of a young girl with frizzy dark hair veiling her face. She is running a finger across my palm, drawing lines that may or may not be there, proclaiming the end of my life at thirty-two. Then she looks up at me, the hair falling away from her face and fading into a strawberry blonde. She smiles and I recognize her pale blue eyes and thin lips. She is me.

Jenna Austin serves us spaghetti with meatballs in a bowl large enough to fit on my head. It is more than I will be able to eat, but I'm pleased to have been invited for dinner.

We sit in the living room, in front of the television. This room, like the rest of the house, is an homage to falconry. Behind Tom there's a carefully crafted wooden case with glass doors and a collection of some fifty hoods inside. They are carefully stored away from the dust and grime of a busy falconry home, but also placed appropriately to be admired. Hoods cannot be mass produced. They are too specific to bird size and almost always custom-made to order. Falconers like Tom who have flown falconry birds for decades have huge collections to rifle through in an emergency or a pinch. We call our hoods by the last name of the man who made them, Rollins, Helsom, Maynes, and every one is unique. Most are gorgeously crafted.

Tom is surrounded by dogs, two Springer spaniels and an Elhew pointer. They all work in the field. They are all adored. All three are hoping for scraps, but seem to know better than to pester me. Tom has an eye on them.

Jenna brings me a beer and settles in at last to eat some of the meal she's made. I rarely see her sitting still. She is always feeding birds or bustling to be a better hostess, her long dark pony tail swinging behind her pretty face and amazing smile.

"What kind of duck is that?" I ask, pointing at a mount of a small drake and hen.

"Bufflehead," Tom says. "Very hard to catch."

"Rat bastards," Jenna says fondly.

"They around here?" I ask, thinking I would love to see some. The drake is a beautiful duck, black and white, compact build and iridescent head.

"You'll see them from time to time, but good luck getting them off the water," he says. I think that I would still love to see some, that there are still many duck species I've yet to see. Every species is different, has their own tricks and particular beauty. Hunting ducks with a falcon is much more than I imagined.

"You're having a pretty good season," he says in a noncommittal tone.

"Rough start. A set back or two," I say.

"You feeling better?" Jenna asks and I give her my most reassuring smile and a nod. She worries over everyone.

"You've caught more ducks than most anyone else this season with a first-year bird."

I nod, not sure what to say. We're out there trying anyway and I've made a lot of mistakes. It's amazing I didn't lose my falcon for good. I don't think I should be bragging.

"How did you get into falconry?" Tom asks.

"My grandfather," I say, and tell him the story of the falcon on the roof.

"Where did you grow up?" Tom asks, and takes another bite of his spaghetti.

"Riverside," I say and Tom puts the fork down in his bowl. He looks thoughtful and I lean forward because I think this conversation is about to get interesting.

"What year would that have been?" he asks, giving me his full attention and a serious expression.

I do the math in my head, adding years to 1971 when I was born. "I think '79, maybe '80," I say.

"Not a lot of us flying falcons around here those years," he says. "It was probably my bird, probably my peregrine." He nods as if satisfied and twirls another forkful of spaghetti.

I stare at him for moment, my mouth agape, but I don't say anything. What's there to say? Of course it was his falcon.

At Whitewater Ranch the sun is starting to peek over the windmills to the east. The turbines are just barely starting to churn in the air. Some mornings are torn apart by a gale and some are perfectly calm. I haven't been able to figure out which days will be gritty with the rough wind, but I've been watching for hints and portents. I'll decipher the clues and learn to predict.

There are only a couple of days left in the season, and I turned thirty-three two days ago. I can run now as well as I did when I was still chasing after a wayward falcon. Today, Anakin is in the air waiting on at a thousand feet. I was thinking this would be the last Whitewater hunt for the season, but I was hoping to catch Butch out here. I don't see his truck anywhere.

The pond is packed with ducks. Surely a few will panic and I won't need help flushing. It was just that I wanted to wish him a good summer. Next year we will be back, but the falcon will look different. Anakin will moult out his first-year feathers over the summer. His primary wing feathers and tail feathers will come in a little shorter and that will make him a little faster, a little more maneuverable. His colors will brighten, the brown exchanged for peach and blue-black. He will look like a different bird. I wonder if I will I look different too.

At the edge of the pond, I splash through the water, my Sorels kicking up a sparkling spray while a wave of ducks rises into the desert air. They twist and turn, a single fluid being evading the trajectory of a falling peregrine.

Woman the Hunter

"What's he doing?" my mom asks.

"What does it look like he's doing?" I reply.

"It looks like he's sitting on a pole." My mom laughs as I glare at the falcon.

The falcon is perched above a transformer, balancing on the creosote-stained wood between the wires and staring across the desert toward Palm Springs. He should be climbing the sky, positioning himself for the hunt, but instead he's sight-seeing from a one-hundred-foot pole. In front of him, in the distance, the windmill behemoths are starting to churn. There are nearly four thousand of them spaced carefully across the landscape; right now all of them are facing east, preparing for the morning gusts. I figure we've got about a half an hour before the Whitewater breeze turns into a falcon-tossing gale and it doesn't look like the falcon cares.

He's splitting his interest between the ducks in the pond and the two women before him. To me it looks like he's more interested in us, a redhead and a brunette that look nothing alike, but share blood and secrets. I wonder what the falcon is thinking and though I'll never know, I imagine him ponder-ing human relationships. I wouldn't put it past him. In his own way he knows more about desire, determination, and loyalty than he will be able to teach me in his lifetime. Sometimes I think he knows me better than I know myself.

My mom is wearing her good shoes, a white quilted sweat-shirt, a huge smile, and they're all new to me. This is the first time she's ever been to visit me anywhere. I know her voice over the phone, but I'm not intimately familiar with her ward-robe or the way thoughts flash across her face. I guess that's why I didn't believe her last night when she insisted on joining the hunt. I guess that's why I'm surprised by her genuine inter-est in my hunting grounds, but the falcon is giving her time to take it all in.

Still, I really wish Anakin would demonstrate something like I've described over the phone. I've told my mom this is spiritual, life-changing, breathtaking, but all we're doing is waiting on a perched peregrine. Watching him watching us while the morning grows old is hardly transformative, but my mom doesn't seem to notice.

"So this is Whitewater," she says as she pivots and takes in every direction, nodding with approval.

"Yeah, this is it." I follow her gaze and smile. This place is sacred and I'm relieved that I didn't have to tell her that. "I just wish Butch was still here."

"The caretaker?" she asks.

"Yeah, the one I told you looked like a tall Yosemite Sam." I laugh and imagine his serious face cracked into a friendly grin. I don't know where Butch went, but the cattle are gone from the ranch and he left with them, an old cowboy follow-ing his herd. I suppose he told me all I needed to know about Whitewater, how to get through the hole in the fence, where to watch for eagles, when to look for teal. Still, I wish I knew where find him. I would like to say thank you one more time.

Whitewater Ranch still belongs to the Bureau of Land Management, but I love to imagine its earlier days, that the rancher dug the pond at the northeast end of the property on what must have been faith. It's a beautiful place, but nothing has ever looked more like the desert. Small dunes shift in the constant wind and the never-ending creosote is no harbinger of water. The plants clone themselves instead of chancing seeds and exert their energy instead on roots so ancient, tangled, and deep that a sip of water is a certainty.

Maybe it was a wet year and the rancher examined the ephemeral Whitewater Creek running and proclaimed it a sign. Maybe he had a Cahuilla friend who could hear it raging as a river somewhere beneath the sand. Either way he was a determined man to make this oasis rise out of the desert's fringe.

Although I would rather think the rancher was not a cowboy at all, but a medicine woman. Maybe that's why the pond filled and the cattle grew fat. Then when the railroad came through with a thirst to quench, she was able to barter water for railroad ties and enclosed her pastures with fences that would still stand today.

Maybe she saw into the future and imagined the two other ponds that would be cut into the earth. She would know that this water would save the hillsides from a raging fire in the heat of the summer. The ponds would prevent the flames from licking the ranch off the land for good. She wouldn't be able to imagine the great metal birds that extinguished the blaze; vertical flight wouldn't be possible until the thirties. Instead, she might have had a vision of my mother and I, one hundred years later, standing beneath a stubborn peregrine, facing the wind, waiting for his wings to lift.

Butch gave me permission to fly the falcon on this land leased from the government. Now that he's gone we're trespassing. Any moment a ranger might drive by. The ranger will be angry and the ticket will be more than I can afford, but this is my land now and I'll keep coming back.

"Mom, there's a white truck coming. Duck down." We dip behind a berm, alternately glancing at the falcon and the truck. It isn't a ranger, but we stay hidden, smiling at one another.

I'm ten years old and digging through the dark rectangular bin that holds the trash in my father's office. This is the only way I can find out what he is doing with his days and what he might be thinking about his future. What I really want to know is if sometime I might fit into it, if somewhere between managing a grocery store and going to law school, he might want to be a father too. I know he has a girlfriend; I found a note she left behind in the junk drawer. Maybe she will want to meet me. Maybe my dad will want to show her what a good father he is and he will be sitting with her by the pool the next time I come. Maybe he will introduce me as his daughter for once instead of his housekeeper, which I guess is supposed to be funny. I've never found it funny.

I come to clean his house once a week, but he's never here. He's a ghost that I can only get to know through the clues of a dusty house. I work through the house cleaning one countertop at time, rationing the drawers that I rummage through and the cabinets that might contain new things while I scrub. I always save the trash can in the office for last, after the kitchen floor has been mopped and the living room vacuumed. Sometimes there is a postcard in the bin and that's what I'm looking for now. Mainly I find paid bills, catalogues, and disappointment, but today I find one at the bottom, flat and un-

soiled as if he threw it away immediately. I close my eyes, trying to savor the moment.

I guess the date to make the anticipation last longer, maybe next weekend, I think. Then I open my eyes and read the round cursive that I've learned to recognize as my mom's. "Dear Barry, I would like to pick up Becky on January 26th, the weekend before her birthday." Two weeks from now.

I put the card back in the trash and carry the whole lot outside to empty it into the bigger can. I squeal and dance a little, trying to get the excitement out my system. Only two weeks from now. Before I go back across the street to my grandparents I have to be composed, quiet, and unaffected. I breathe deep and chew on my lip. It's a happy secret, but I have to bury it.

My grandmother always refuses to tell me when my mom is coming to get me, because she says I get too wound up. If anyone finds out I can read my future in my father's trash, they will put a stop to it. Then there will nothing to look forward to, no more fantasies about time spent with my mom. Even though my daydreaming never quite fleshes out into the present, it's all I have.

The reality is that my stepfather will monitor my every moment with my mother and be certain that his own children are always included. Then my grandparents will quiz me on the details of the weekend and betray me to my father if I do anything unapproved. My father will make demands on what I can and cannot do in my mother's company and I never have her to myself. It's only in my found treasure that I read my mom's desire to include me, for a moment alone with me, and for a future of shared memories that belong to us alone. It's too dangerous to keep the cards, but I memorize them and reread them over and over in my mind.

Last night my mom arrived with a bottle of Yellowtail merlot. Walking around my house with filled glasses, we talked about the details someone had lovingly designed in 1925 when they built my house, about the touches I would add to it in the future. "This is nice, Becky."

"There still a lot of work to do," I note and gesture at the unpainted linen cabinet with the missing door.

"There's always a lot of work to do," she agrees. We share a grin and migrate to the kitchen.

"So you're talking to Adam again?" She asks this knowing the answer.

"I am," I say. I don't know if we'll be able to start over. It doesn't make a difference that I was right. It only matters that he got out, but it's changed us both. You don't get back exactly what you've lost. I pour another glass of wine for myself and smile at my mother.

My mother never came to visit me during the four years I lived in Florida, or when I went away to college, or when I lived in Australia for a brief time. We've always sipped our wine over the phone. Now I have my mom to myself, in the house I just bought where the falcon sleeps in a small room off the kitchen. I watch her smile over the rim of my glass and feel giddy.

"You know I've driven all over California in the last year," my mom says. Her mouth and eyes are shaped into a wonderful combination of surprise and smugness. "Clyde never let me go anywhere."

"Well, you can go anywhere you want now."

"I know. I can come to see you anytime I want." She sounds thrilled. I nod my agreement and don't say a word. I don't have to. "Are you flying Anakin in the morning?"

"At the crack of dawn," I answer.

"I want to come," she says.

"Are you sure? You don't have to. I won't be gone long."

"Absolutely, I'm sure," she answers.

My mom points in the direction of the pond and asks if that is where the water is. I nod to her and explain that we have to wait to walk over so we don't flush the ducks before the falcon is in the air.

"I think I hear them," my mom says with her ear cocked into the wind.

"Hear what?" I ask.

"The ducks." She shushes me and concentrates. "Yep, I hear them."

She looks so focused and earnest that I don't laugh. "You don't hear them, Mom. They're ringnecks."

"What do you mean?" she asks.

With the sun stretching over the top of the berm, our faces begin to warm and I explain. mallards quack, but there are no mallards in the pond. Duck noises are soft and subtle. They have private conversation mostly and don't announce their presence like a songbird. Widgeon have a sweet whistle that could easily lull you to sleep, but you have to listen close or press them under a falcon to hear to it. Ringnecks, small diving ducks that swim as well as they fly, make hardly a sound. They focus all their energy into their wings instead of their voices. The only ringbill noise I know by heart is the whir of their fast wingbeat.

"What's that I hear now?" my mom asks, still concentrating. I listen and grin.

"My favorite sound, the falcon's bell." I find him and point into the sky. "Look, he's in the air." The bell on his ankle is doing its job, ringing out the beat of his wings, and helping me locate his position. He's just starting to climb into the air, racing down the breeze and then turning into it to utilize the lift.

"It's windy. He's getting blown around a little," my mom notes.

"That's okay. We love a little wind," I reply.

Whitewater is the mouth of the desert, where the Santa Ana winds are first exhaled. The ranch is nestled in the San Gorgonio Pass, an opening cut through the two peaks of Mt. San Gorgonio to the north and Mt. San Jacinto to the southeast by the San Andreas and San Jacinto fault lines. Nothing about this place is stable. It was created by shaky ground and unstable air.

This is the place in California where the ocean air collides with the desert heat. Everyday there's a battle between worlds as the air pressure equalizes and the tussle produces wind. In the morning it blows from east and the desert wins. In the evening the moist Pacific air triumphs and the winds switch, raging from the west. Neither side ever wins permanently, but they do battle three hundred days a year.

The Whitewater River falls from the mountains and whispers nearly hidden through the sand. I know it's there, but almost never hear it over the wind battling through the creosote. The squeeze through the mountains and the trickle of the water urge sixty-nine million birds a year past the windmills in the fall and spring. I know this is an oasis and the tumult feels familiar and comfortable.

No other falconers hunt this pond. The devil winds make them nervous. Their falcons don't take well to the raucous air. I've learned to turn my face east to blow stray hair from my eyes and the falcon has learned to pump his wings toward the sunrise. Whitewater has become our bread and butter, the best place to hunt, the land that feels like home. The other falconers think we're in exile in the desert and I used to think so too, but I know the wind now, the white sand that warms it, and the pattern of the ducks migrating through the pass.

The falcon is climbing steadily and I count off the invisible markers of height to my mom. "He's at five hundred feet. Let's start walking toward the pond."

"Won't the ducks flush?"

"Not with a falcon above them, Mom. That narrow-winged silhouette means winged executioner. They're born knowing that. Our job is to be scarier than the falcon."

"Do you think he'll fly off?" she asks.

"I hope not." I stop to count how many fly-offs now in these first two seasons, ten or twelve perhaps, and laugh a little. It's been months since he's flown away. "I doubt he's going anywhere this time, though."

"I thought he used to fly off a lot," she says.

"He did, but that was the fly-off pond, not Whitewater," I answer.

"Hence the name. Does he still fly off there?" She laughs as she asks and I try to laugh too, but I can't.

"It's gone now, Mom. The fly-off pond is a golf course."

The balloon field is gone too, a Super Walmart. As falconers we make places our own with the blood of the game we take and the thanks that we give. We name them so we can speak of them with respect and love them because they share their secrets. We all have our hearts broken bit by bit as the land is sucked into eternal industry. I pray for Whitewater every season and for the hundreds of ducks that use it as a stop over. I

understand, though, how to make new homes. We will all survive when it is gone, but right now we should celebrate it.

"Okay, he's at eight hundred feet. Here's what we're going to
do." I explain to my mom to take the east side of the pond, that
I'll run around to the west. We'll squeeze the ducks to the end
of the pond and get them into the air.

I don't know if this will come together. The truth is that I
never really do. Some of it depends on me, but the falcon, the
ducks, and the desert have their say as well. Every time we all
agree on an outcome it's a gift. It's as if the world says, welcome to the cycle. Surely you belong here. I wonder what this
earthly family of mine will think of my mom.

"What do I do to make the ducks fly?" my mom asks.

I'm already running and don't have time to explain. "Just
do what I do!"

Straddling the pond, my mother and I run on the edges,
but the ducks are swimming placidly, focused on the falcon
above. Anakin is in perfect position, but is looking impatient,
tilting his wings and preparing to jump the gun, dive too soon.
I think that this won't come together, that my mom may not
have it in her to scare up the ducks. I begin to yell and throw
rocks in desperation, but the waterfowl remain unconvinced.

Mom is watching me, thinking. She looks up for the falcon,
finds him and looks back at me. Then she springs into action,
yelling, clapping her hands determinedly.

I remember being three years old, my mother reading to me
from *Winnie-the-Pooh*. I remember that she read to me every
night and tucked me into bed. I can remember her voice, a
serious storyteller getting the facts right with her careful in-

flections. When I learned to read I imagined her voice as I sounded out the words in my head.

I asked her last night if she remembered reading to me. I asked if it really was *Winnie-the-Pooh* that she read. She nodded and took a sip of wine.

"Yes, I read that to you, but Becky, I only read it once. It must have been when I was having a moment of trying to be a good mother. I thought I should read to you every night, but I only did it that one time."

I see my mom raging at the ducks for the sake of my falcon and think that this memory will be a similar one. That from this point forward the recollection of my mom trying to flush ducks for me will multiply into as many hunts as I need her to be with me. Then my mom roars, firmly planting her foot into the pond and the sound of feathers overpowers the wind. All twenty of the ducks rise into the sky. I'm racing behind them, ensuring they don't drop back into the water, and as they clear the pond, a dark streak rips through the flock and a ringbill falls to the ground.

I call out our success as I sprint to find the falcon and help him, but when I get there he's got everything under control. He looks calm and regal, glancing up only to acknowledge my presence and then going back to his meal. It's late in the season and this will be one of the last in a handful of hunts we have left. I think about how far we've come in our relationship and wonder how much further there might be to go.

My mom walks up from the distance and I examine the scene at my feet. The ringbill is dead, but its blood is pooling into the sand, the desert taking back its portion. I touch the duck, naming it, Drake Ringbill and thanking it. I turn to face Mom as she draws closer and warn her off. "It's a bloody mess, Mom."

"I know, but I want to see." She looks down and nods, but doesn't flinch. "They all came off. All of the ducks flushed."

"They did. You're a good duck flusher, Mom."

"I stepped in the water," she says and points to her good shoes. She's wet to the ankle, sand clinging to her shoe and pant leg.

I wince.

"It's okay, they'll dry," she assures me.

"You took one for the team. Good job." I smile up at her and step the falcon onto my glove for some quail from my pocket. Then I slip the ringbill into my vest. I stand so we can both admire the peregrine eating his victory meal. "Did you see it?" I ask.

My mom explains that when the ducks came off she stopped and watched them rise. She says she knew if she watched the ducks the falcon would soon come into view. She saw him careen into the flock, his target already chosen, and pluck a meal from the sky.

"The killing doesn't bother you?" I ask.

She just shrugs again and I tell her what I saw from my side of the pond. We walk out of the field shoulder to shoulder, retelling our story, adding in details. "You know, Mom, if it were just me alone, they wouldn't have come off, at least not all of them." I tell her this and she smiles. I think to myself that it was a perfect hunt and memorize it like I would a postcard.

Biographical Note

Rebecca K. O'Connor is the author of a novel, *Falcon's Return*, and several reference books on the natural world. She lives in Northern California, sharing her home with Anakin, Ty, and her Brittany spaniel, Booth.